'Why did you [barcode] **she asked.**

He shrugged. 'It's beautiful. I love it, and I thought you might too.'

'I do find it beautiful,' she said.

Then they stood there side by side in silence, looking at the view, hearing distant noises from the innumerable lives below them. Occasionally their shoulders touched.

Jack was indecisive. This was something he wasn't used to. Usually he knew what he wanted, went straight for it. But now he had the feeling that what he did in the next couple of minutes might have unforeseeable consequences. He realised his heart was beating faster. Him, the ice-cool surgeon Jack Sinclair!

Should he kiss her now? He thought she'd like it, suspected she wanted to be kissed. But he also knew that one kiss would start an entire new relationship between them. And the thought both worried and excited him. All the rules he had been living his life by broken. But with Miranda, he couldn't help himself...

Dear Reader

A year ago I wrote three books—A VERY SPECIAL MIDWIFE, A CHILD TO CALL HER OWN, and THE NOBLE DOCTOR. They were about life in a maternity unit in a large city hospital, the Dell Owen. I was really pleased at the number of letters I received saying how much readers had enjoyed the Dell Owen trilogy, and asking was there any chance of any more? No need to ask; I love writing about maternity. So now we have another three.

My daughter is a midwife. She supplies me with the technical details for my stories, and the feelings that nurses, doctors, midwives have about their profession. They are trained not to let their feelings show—but they are there, especially in a life-enhancing department like Maternity.

These three books are about two brothers and a sister, all working together in the Dell Owen Hospital. Jack, Toby and Carly are vastly different in character, united in their love for each other, but feel that sibling rivalry that is a part of so many high-achieving families. All three fall in love—though '*the course of true love never did run smooth*'.

I hope you get as much pleasure from reading about the Dell Owen Hospital staff as I get from writing about them. **Look out for Toby's story, coming soon in Mills & Boon® Medical Romance™.**

With all good wishes

Gill Sanderson

A SURGEON,
A MIDWIFE:
A FAMILY

BY
GILL SANDERSON

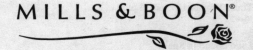

All the characters in this book have no existence outside the imagination of the author, and have no relation whatsoever to anyone bearing the same name or names. They are not even distantly inspired by any individual known or unknown to the author, and all the incidents are pure invention.

First published in Great Britain 2006
Harlequin Mills & Boon Limited,
Eton House, 18-24 Paradise Road, Richmond, Surrey TW9 1SR

© Gill Sanderson 2006

ISBN-13: 978 0 263 84760 4
ISBN-10:   0 263 84760 8

Set in Times Roman 10½ on 13 pt
03-1006-45178

Printed and bound in Spain
by Litografia Rosés, S.A., Barcelona

A SURGEON,
A MIDWIFE:
A FAMILY

Gill Sanderson, aka Roger Sanderson, started writing as a husband-and-wife team. At first Gill created the storyline, characters and background, asking Roger to help with the actual writing. But her job became more and more time-consuming and he took over all of the work. He loves it!

Roger has written many Medical Romance™ books for Harlequin Mills & Boon®. Ideas come from three of his children—Helen is a midwife, Adam a health visitor, Mark a consultant oncologist. Week days are for work; weekends find Roger walking in the Lake District or Wales.

Recent titles by the same author:

A NURSE WORTH WAITING FOR
TELL ME YOU LOVE ME
THE NOBLE DOCTOR*
A CHILD TO CALL HER OWN*
A VERY SPECIAL MIDWIFE*

Dell Owen Maternity

CHAPTER ONE

'Two brothers and a sister. They're known as the good, the bad and the ugly. This one is the ugly one. Jack Sinclair.'

'He's not really ugly,' Miranda said doubtfully, her blue eyes narrowed in contemplation. 'More sort of…craggy.'

'Craggy in behaviour as well as in face,' her new friend Annie Arnold whispered. 'Brilliant neonatal surgeon, there's no doubt about that. If I could get to be half as good as he is, then I'd be very happy. But he's a bit standoffish. For some reason, he doesn't come to parties or anything like that. Polite enough but he keeps his distance. He's been away to America for three weeks, giving lectures, and things have been just a bit more relaxed around here.'

The two of them looked at the tall, green-clad figure who had just entered the operating theatre. First, he went to have a low-voiced conversation with the scrub nurse. Then he straightened, looked round the theatre. Miranda saw an unsmiling face, thoughtful grey eyes that seemed to see everything. The eyes fastened on her, registered that she was a stranger but that she was properly booted, gowned and masked, her short chestnut-brown hair hidden beneath a cap. Then they passed on. In spite of herself, Miranda shivered.

When the figure bent his head again the low buzz of conversation resumed. The patient had not yet been brought in, she was outside being given a last check by the anaesthetist.

'Is he married? Children of his own?' Miranda asked. She was curious about this aloof man.

'Neither married nor attached to anyone. So far as we know, that is. A couple of people have indicated quite clearly that if he wanted company, they were available. You know, for a drink at the Red Lion or an evening at the hospital social club. And he's turned them down. Politely but definitely.'

'He won't mind me being in his theatre?'

Annie shook her head. 'Not at all. Look, as well as me there's another two SHOs here. If he thinks you're here to learn, that's fine. The odd thing is, he's a very good teacher. It's just that…when he's teaching you, you feel that he has no interest in you at all. No interest beyond you as a medical professional. He's just so…detached.'

There was a stirring in the room as the patient was wheeled in. A baby, a beautiful little girl. Miranda looked at the tiny body and gave an involuntary shudder. It seemed wrong that someone so small as this should have to have surgery.

The surgeon looked up. 'Our patient is Chloe Metcalfe. She has oesophageal atresia—a blockage in the oesophagus—that ends in a blind pouch. There is no way food can reach the stomach. However, there is a fistula into the trachea. We have checked with X-rays and echocardiograph. There is no evidence in this case of cardiac anomaly. Often, there is. I shall open the chest and connect the two sections. Now, stand where you can see but not interfere with our work.'

His voice was as formidable as his appearance. It was deep, clear, and Miranda thought it could be musical. But instead it was distant. There was no friendliness.

People shuffled forward. Miranda did, too, and discovered that her eyes were teeming with tears. It was not apprehension or fear, just that she was not yet fully used to her new contact lenses.

Perhaps she was just a little nervous. Jack Sinclair wasn't the most welcoming person she'd ever met. But mostly it was the contact lenses. Whatever it was, she tripped. Without thinking, she stretched out her hand to save herself. And her naked hand landed on the tray of instruments that the scrub nurse had just unwrapped. The instruments weren't sterile any more. They couldn't be used.

'Oh I'm sorry,' Miranda gasped. 'I…I slipped.'

She was aware of how feeble her explanation sounded. And the silence around her grew and grew.

'Send a runner for a new tray of instruments,' Jack Sinclair said to the scrub nurse. Then, after more heart-stopping silence, he turned his icy gaze on Miranda. 'You are?'

'Midwife Miranda Gale.'

'What are you doing in my theatre?'

'I'm here to observe. I want… I want…to learn.'

'Very commendable. So far, in your training, have you learned anything about the absolute importance of keeping instruments sterile? Of keeping bare hands away from them?'

'Yes, I have. I'm sorry I slipped, it was an accident.'

'Accidents only happen because people let them happen. Now, keep out of my way, stand back where you can do no more harm. I'll want to speak to you later.'

What was so awful was the fact the he didn't seem angry with her. She could have accepted anger from him, felt even that she deserved it. That would have been the reaction of one person to another. But somehow he hadn't even reacted to her humanity. He had been perfectly polite, but his chilly detachment had made her feel like a non-person. Just like Annie had said.

She knew she had no right to, but Miranda felt a little angry herself.

Still, she was here to learn. The runner returned with a fresh tray of instruments, the scrub nurse unwrapped them and put them ready. Once again Miranda looked at Chloe, dwarfed by the chromed equipment of the anaesthetist. Most of her tiny body was swathed in green drapes but there was that bared patch of pink skin, surely too small for any kind of incision.

Without looking, the surgeon stretched out his hand and the scrub nurse placed a scalpel in it. Obviously these two had worked together before. A moment's pause. Miranda could tell by the hunched body, the bent head, that he was focussing, directing all his concentration on the task in hand. Then the first confident cut, and Jack Sinclair began to speak. 'OK, everyone, pay attention, please.'

He was still in his green scrubs, but had taken off his mask and his cap. Rather to her surprise, Miranda saw that his hair was longer than she would have expected, dark and slightly curly. But the rest of his face matched his stormy grey eyes. As she had said to Annie, it was craggy. There were the high cheekbones, the well-defined jaw line. And it didn't look as if he smiled much.

'You wanted to speak to me,' she said.

'I did, Miranda. I've never seen you before. Why is that?'

'Well, you haven't seen me before because I've just started at the hospital. I'm…I'm on the bank.'

'So you've just started and you're a bank nurse?' His voice was totally without inflection. Miranda felt a thrill of dismay, there could be a hidden threat here. As a bank nurse she was paid by the shift. There was no continuity, no guarantee of full-time work, she was sent for when she was needed. If a consultant said that he wasn't satisfied with her, there would be no more work offered.

'I'm hoping to be made permanent eventually,' she said. After a very exhaustive interview, Jenny Donovan, the head of midwifery, had told her that there should be more than enough work for her. And in time there was the promise of a proper staff job.

'I see. Where did you do your training?'

Miranda told him about the small hospital in East Yorkshire where she had been so happy.

'I know of the place, it's very good in its way— but here it is different. You are working for the obs and gynae section. That's fine. But I'm part of a sub-section, here we are a tertiary unit for neonatal surgery. There's only a handful of these in the country. And I want the standards here to be as high as anywhere. So. You told me you were in my theatre to learn. Anything else?'

'Yes, later I'll be specialling Chloe Metcalfe, the little girl you've just operated on. When she comes out of the post-op room and goes down to SCBU this afternoon, I'll be looking after her.'

'I see. O and G can spare you just to observe an operation?'

This was the embarrassing bit. 'I don't officially start work till this afternoon. I…er, came in on my own time.'

'Did you indeed?'

This obviously surprised him a little and just for a moment Miranda thought she saw the faint glimmer of approval in his eyes. But it was quickly gone.

She had never met anyone who seemed so distant. Perhaps if she apologised again…? 'May I say that I'm very sorry that I tripped and contaminated your instrument tray. But I've just started wearing contact lenses and at times I—'

'Miranda, you know that's no concern of mine. What is my concern is that there could have been an accident in my theatre. But I'm sure you've learned from your mistake.'

'Yes,' she mumbled.

'Good. The matter is now closed. Now, what was the operation you've just observed?'

She looked at him, perplexed. 'Why, it was for oesophageal atresia. You said so.'

'True. And what specific nursing techniques will you need to use after this operation?'

'Are you questioning my nursing skills? I can assure you that I—'

'I am just ensuring that the child I have just operated on gets the best of care.'

She couldn't argue with that. 'Well, apart from the usual obs I should ensure that the child remained prone, with the head up, resting at an angle of between thirty and sixty degrees.'

'And?'

'There must be frequent suction of the oesophagus.'

He nodded. 'That is satisfactory. You seem both competent and interested.' He turned to a locker, took out a pen and pad and scribbled something on it. Then he handed a sheet to her. 'That is the name of a very good textbook and page references to this condition. If you care to look them up, you might find them useful.'

This was totally unexpected. Why should he go to this trouble for her? 'Why...why, thank you. It's good of you to help me.'

'I'm not helping you, I'm helping the hospital. That is part of my job. Now, good morning, Miranda.'

She had been dismissed. 'Good morning,' she said, and walked away.

It took her a while before she worked out exactly why she was so angry with Jack Sinclair. She accepted that he was entitled to be angry with her—she knew surgeons who would have ordered her out of the theatre at once, and then afterwards given her a full-scale dressing-down. And she would have taken it. She had made a mistake.

But this one had neither ordered her out nor dressed her down. Well, not much. In fact, he had tried to help her, which somehow made things worse.

Then she realised why she was angry. There had been no recognition of her as a person in her own right, with a personality. She didn't want this man to fall for her or pay her compliments, she just wanted some acknowledgement that she was a person, not just a hospital employee. All it needed was a smile, a look even, perhaps a small shared joke or some comment about the weather. And she had got nothing.

Jack Sinclair was not to know, but she had come to a new hospital, a new city, to start a new life. Her old life was wrecked and her old ambitions now impossible. At times there was a dreadful feeling that she was only half a woman. Now she had to stand up for herself, the alternative was despair. She would not be bullied or browbeaten by anyone.

The trouble was, Jack Sinclair had neither bullied nor

browbeaten her. He had treated her with perfect courtesy. But for him, she was just another colleague. Miranda Gale the person didn't exist. And for some reason—possibly sheer cussedness—Miranda also wanted him to know she was a woman.

Later there was time for a coffee with Annie before she had to start work. Over the past fortnight the two had quickly become friends. Miranda had come to Liverpool's Dell Owen Hospital in late October, thinking that all possible flats, bedsitters, nurses' rooms would already be let. But there had been an advert on the hospital notice-board. *Half-share in flat, own bedroom, non-smoker, convenient for hospital.* And she and Annie had instantly got on.

'How'd you get on with craggy Jack Sinclair?' Annie asked. She put two large milky coffees on the canteen table, handed Miranda a large sticky bun and sat down, her green eyes sparkling with curiosity.

Miranda shrugged, took a sugar-laden mouthful. 'He was like you said. Polite but distant. And he gave me some reading to look up. Is he always like that?'

'Always. But there are people in the know who insist that he's the man to operate on their children. We get plenty from London and so on, and we've had patients from both continental Europe and America.'

'I see.' Miranda didn't want to know just how good Jack was. 'You said there are three of them—the good the bad and the ugly. If he's the ugly, who's the good and the bad?'

A faint touch of red tinged Annie's cheeks. 'Well, the other two are twins—Toby and Carly. They're both SHOs and they're both in the department. You'll meet them soon enough. Carly is the good. She's quiet, gets on with her job, everybody likes her. Toby is the bad. He's gorgeous-looking, has a joke for everyone, is everyone's friend.'

'So why bad?'

'He's a heart-breaker. I don't think he means to be but he is. He's not really bad, he never encourages anyone, never promises anything he doesn't mean.' Annie grinned. 'I think the feeling among the younger women in the hospital is that for someone as good-looking as Toby to be unattached is a bit of a cheek.'

'Do I take it that this experience is personal?' Miranda asked.

'No, not at all. Well, not really. Two dates and we both agreed that was it. He couldn't have been fairer or nicer.'

'Doesn't sound like his brother. Tell me more about Jack Sinclair.'

Annie drank her coffee then said, 'The two men couldn't be more different. Jack is the older brother. And he cuts the twins no slack at all. He's tough on all us SHOs but he's tougher on those two.' She shook her head in exasperation. 'Like I said, he's a brilliant surgeon, he's a brilliant teacher. But he keeps everyone at a distance. He rarely asks about your private life. He's the strong, silent type.'

'And you say he's not married? He could be…quite attractive.' Miranda felt a small thrill as she admitted this.

'Not married or engaged and never goes out with anyone from the hospital. Sometimes we see pictures of him in the local paper, escorting some glamorous woman somewhere. But nothing seems to come of it.'

'That figures,' Miranda muttered.

It was work that Miranda loved. She was specialling baby Chloe, checking her vital signs, administering her medication, perhaps providing that love that even the tiniest neonate seemed able to sense. For once there were no parents, no relations. Chloe's mother was still in the post-labour ward, her father was hurrying home from an oil rig off the African coast.

They were alone in a side ward, the intensive care room of SCBU. And Miranda was happy. She made sure the baby was comfortable, checked the drips, did the fifteen-minute obs. All work she had done before, work at which she was expert.

Chloe started to cry, a weak, kitten-like wailing that was all her tiny vocal cords could manage. Miranda waited a minute or two to see if her charge would nod off to sleep again. But no. She was in pain. This was to be expected and the surgeon—Jack—had written out a prescription for a painkiller. Carefully, Miranda administered it by the syringe driver. Then she waited.

Five minutes later Chloe was still crying, and if anything seemed to be in even more pain. Miranda waited another five minutes and the crying still hadn't stopped. Chloe was now showing signs of exhaustion, there was a limit to the amount of crying a baby could do. But the pain was obviously still there.

In her previous hospital Miranda would have increased the dosage of painkiller and then asked a doctor to sign the prescription. She suspected that Jack might not approve of this and so went to find a SHO to fill out the form. And right outside the side ward, purely by chance, she ran into Jack.

So far she had only seen him in scrubs. Now he was in full consultant mode—beautifully cut black suit, pristine white shirt and the college of surgeons' tie. He looked more unapproachable than ever.

He nodded to her, politely but coolly, and prepared to pass. Miranda decided she didn't want to be passed.

'Mr Sinclair, Baby Chloe is crying and distressed. I think perhaps she needs more painkiller. I was going to find a SHO but since you're here and if you're not too busy…'

A change in his face. A small wrinkle between his eyes. He was thinking. And an expression of…concern?

'I'm never too busy to look after one of my charges, Miranda. Let's go and see.'

Miranda blinked as she followed him into the side ward. This was a slightly different Jack Sinclair. He seemed…a bit warmer. Maybe she'd imagined it.

The two of them stood side by side, looking at Chloe in her incubator. Miranda was interested to see that he looked at the baby before asking her for the notes. Thinking of the baby as a person rather than a case.

'How long has she been crying?'

'For ten minutes now. The crying is getting weaker but I think that's because she's losing strength.'

He didn't answer at once, but stared at the infant for a few moments more. Then he slid a hand inside the incubator, and with a forefinger stroked aside a tiny wisp of hair from Chloe's forehead. It was a gentle, delicate act.

'I think you're right. He took up a prescription form and quickly wrote on it. 'Give her another five mil. You're an experienced and competent children's nurse. If she's still crying in…how long, Miranda?'

He was asking her opinion? Not like some other surgeons she had met. 'If she's still crying in another five minutes, I'd be concerned,' Miranda said.

'Good. I agree. I can't stay, I have a list waiting for me, but if Chloe here is still crying in five minutes, find an SHO and suggest to him that he contacts the duty registrar. Tell him that it was my suggestion.'

He turned to go. Quickly, Miranda asked, 'Um, how did you know that I was a competent and experienced children's nurse? I introduced myself as a midwife.'

She had graduated as a midwife and then spent a further two years gaining the additional children's nurse qualification.

He looked at her, his expression unreadable. 'I phoned and asked Jenny Donovan about you.' Then he left, leaving Miranda in a state of confusion.

It happened entirely by accident.

Miranda was visiting the Landmoss Clinic, part of the Dell Owen Hospital outreach programme. The clinic was in a brand-new building six miles from the main hospital and catered for simple obs and gynae cases, as well as having a couple of children's wards. Serious cases were, of course, referred to the main hospital, but the Landmoss had a growing reputation among the local population.

She wasn't even there to work, well, not properly. She had just finished an early shift, ending it in Jenny Donovan's office, talking about future work. Jenny had picked up a packet from her desk and let out a sigh of dismay. 'These X-rays should have gone to Landmoss. And they'll be needed this afternoon.'

Miranda, having finished work, had the afternoon free and had offered to take the package. 'It'll be good for me to go,' she had said to Jenny. 'I fancy a look round the clinic.'

'Thanks, Miranda, you're an angel.' Jenny smiled gratefully. 'I'll phone and say that you're on your way.'

So here she was at the Landmoss. It looked a happy, cared-for building. And the minute she entered reception she heard shrieks of childish laughter. Quite a few children were obviously having a lot of fun.

She was met by Dr Tom Ramsey, who beamed at her, said he was very grateful, grabbed the packet of X-rays and said that he was busy at the moment but that Molly Jowett, the receptionist, would show her around. Miranda liked the friendly staff at once.

Molly, a cheerful, slim brunette, smiled. 'First come and have a peek in Kingfisher Ward,' she said. 'We're having a bit of a party. One of our patients is seven—so that's our excuse.'

So Miranda went to peek into Kingfisher Ward. This was where the howls of laughter were coming from.

She thought there was something wonderfully appealing about the sound of children laughing, the complete unselfconsciousness of it. And these were ill children. Just for a moment sadness overwhelmed her—but then she thrust it back. She was a professional.

'No need to let them know we're here,' Molly whispered. 'You can meet them all later.' So the pair of them peered through the half-open door.

There were children and a handful of mothers. Some kind of game was going on. Each child in turn had to creep near a bed. And when he or she got too close, a roaring but friendly looking lion would leap from under the bed. Afterwards, it promptly collapsed on the floor. Then, greatly daring, the child had to climb onto the back of the lion—which promptly woke up and was forced to canter round the ward.

'That man's going to be tired when he finishes,' Molly said. 'But the kids are really enjoying themselves. I wish I'd brought my camera, I'd love a picture or two.'

'There's a camera in my car,' said Miranda. 'I'll get it.'

She fetched the camera, took a good dozen pictures. No one noticed them at the door as everyone was too busy enjoying themselves.

'This nearly didn't happen,' Molly said. 'We organised the outfit and one of the dads was coming to be our lion but he had to cry off only just an hour ago. Work wouldn't let him go. Tom has a list of appointments, he just couldn't cancel them. And then…'

But Miranda had noticed something. From under the lion's mane, a lock of black hair had escaped. And she caught a glimpse of grey eyes—now circled by bright red make-up. But she recognised those eyes.

It couldn't be! 'That's Jack Sinclair, isn't it?' she asked, trying to keep her voice casual. 'He's a surgeon at the Dell Owen?'

'I believe so. Came here earlier to look at a baby he operated on six months ago, just a check-up. Bit hard for the mum to get to hospital. Then he found out we had no one to play the lion and said he thought he had a couple of hours to spare. Not like any other surgeon I've ever met.'

'He seems to be enjoying himself.'

'Doesn't he just.' Molly chuckled.

Miranda was having difficulty in believing her eyes. Was this the aloof surgeon who kept everyone at a distance? Cavorting on a ward floor dressed as a lion? And, what was more, apparently thoroughly enjoying himself?

'There's another ward next door,' Molly said. 'Cases are a bit more serious there. But the lion's already made a tour. No rides on the back, just a friendly growl or two. Do you want to go into this ward? Have a look around?'

'I wouldn't want to spoil the fun,' Miranda said faintly.

'Well, come this way and I'll show you the maternity section. You might find yourself working here one day.'

Still shocked, Miranda accompanied Molly down a corridor and behind her the sounds of merriment faded. Jack Sinclair? The friendly lion? She couldn't get her mind around it.

Of course, they had to meet. And, either fortunately or unfortunately, they were alone at the time.

After the tour of the clinic Molly took Miranda into the staff lounge to have a coffee together. But Molly was called back to reception and Miranda was left on her own for a while. And into the lounge walked Jack.

Somewhere he had changed out of his lion costume. Now he was dressed just in a white shirt and the black suit trousers; tie and jacket were both over his arm. And he looked…tousled. His hair needed combing, his newly washed face was brighter than she remembered. The cool, aloof consultant had gone. Here was a totally different man.

Miranda grinned. She was going to enjoy herself. 'You make a wonderful lion, Mr Sinclair,' she said.

He looked at her, horrified. 'Miranda. What are you doing here?'

'Just a passing visit. It's not impossible that I could work here some time. I must say, the atmosphere here is much less formal than in hospital. Consultants dressed as lions hiding under beds?'

He threw his jacket over a chair, walked to the quietly bubbling coffee-machine and poured himself a cup. He was recovering now. 'Since you have me at a disadvantage, you can call me Jack,' he said.

'Jack it is. Do you often get to play a lion—Jack?'

'Seldom. In fact, I've never done it before.'

'Did you enjoy it?'

He came to sit opposite her, coffee-mug in his hand. So far she had seen him dressed in scrubs and in his immaculate black suit. On each occasion he had looked the perfect professional. Now he looked casual. Now she saw Jack the man, not a professional hiding behind a kind of uniform. And with a sudden lurch inside her, she realised he was very attractive. Not craggy at all.

He smiled, the unexpected change making Miranda's stomach flip. 'I thoroughly enjoyed it. But it was a one-off occasion. I doubt it'll ever happen again.'

'You don't often play with children? You don't like it.'

'I like it,' he admitted, 'and, yes, sometimes I do get to play with them. But never in the main hospital, of course.'

'A pity. But this occasion will be different. We'll have the photographs to remember it by.'

His face changed. 'Photographs, Miranda?'

Suddenly somewhat nervous, she took out her digital camera. 'I was just outside the door when you were doing your act. Molly said it would be great if we had some pictures. I had my camera in the car so I fetched it and took a few shots.'

She handed the camera to him. 'Look in that little screen, flick that button and you can see the pictures I took.'

He peered at the shots she had taken. His face had taken on that closed expression she had now seen so often. An expression that told her nothing of his thoughts. Then he held the camera in one hand, touched it reflectively with a finger. 'I didn't know I was being photographed,' he said.

She watched him anxiously as he turned her camera over, looking at the controls. 'I hope you're not going to try to wipe the pictures out,' she said. 'Quite a few children—and mothers—will be disappointed if you do.'

He handed the camera to her. 'I wouldn't want to disappoint any children,' he said. 'And I wouldn't dream of interfering with what is not my property. I take it that the photographs will only be available here in Landmoss?'

She held the camera up to her eye, flicked through the shots she had taken. There was one of the lion raising a paw, gathering itself ready to leap. Even under the make-up, the face was clearly recognisable. Jack Sinclair, the surgeon. Miranda showed the shot to him.

'I like this one best,' she said casually. 'I thought of having a big print made—about twelve by eighteen—and pinning it to our notice-board.'

The silence was deafening. 'I don't think I'd care for that,' he said eventually. 'It makes me look a fool.'

'It doesn't make you look a fool! It just shows a side of you that you try to hide. It shows you love children, you like being with them. And you volunteered to do this. It shows that you're willing to join in, let your hair down, relax.'

'Perhaps.'

Miranda took the camera from him. 'I certainly wouldn't put up your picture if you didn't want me to. So I won't. But in return will you do something for me?'

'Blackmail, Miranda? Are you trying to make me do something you suspect I wouldn't want to do?'

She heard the undercurrent of humour in his voice and smiled, but her tone was serious. 'When you talked to me first of all, when I tripped in the theatre, I wouldn't have minded if you'd got mad at me. I deserved it. But you did something perhaps worse. You were cold and distant—didn't seem to recognise that I was a human being. And apparently you treat everyone that way. You're always polite, but you're always…sort of… detached. And I think you should be more friendly.'

His voice was mild. 'It's the way I am, Miranda, the way I like to be. If you're always professional with people, things can't go wrong.'

'What sort of things can go wrong?'

His face was expressionless. 'Personal feelings have no place in a professional relationship.'

'You were having a professional relationship with those children? They seemed to think you were there because you liked them.'

'I did. I do. Miranda, we've only met twice before. You don't know me, I don't know you. So how come I'm feeling I have to justify myself to you?' There was a reluctant smile on his lips as he spoke.

Miranda was wondering the same herself, but she wasn't going to tell him that. She said, 'You're trying to justify yourself to yourself, not me. You won't lose respect, you know. Everyone I've talked to seems to think that you're the best neonatal surgeon in the north of England. Now, are you going to try to be just a bit less forbidding? A bit more open?'

'I suppose the choice is either that or be known throughout the hospital as Jack the lion man,' he muttered. 'Yes, I'll try. I'd prefer not have people talking about me'

They looked at each other in silence. Then Miranda went to the sink in the corner of the room and ran warm water onto a cloth. She came back to face Jack and said, 'You didn't get rid of all your lion make-up. There's a patch of red on your hair, where you can't see it. Would you like me to wipe it away?'

'Please,' he said, after a pause.

He sat still as she dabbed at the red make-up, caught a dribble of water as it ran towards his neck, patted him dry. She was close to him. There was the faint smell of human warmth mixed with some kind of citrusy after-shave. It was incredibly exciting. She could hear, feel his breathing, marked the rise and fall of the powerful chest muscles.

'All done,' she said, after either half a minute or half a day. She didn't want to but she stepped away from him.

'Miranda, meeting you has been quite an experience,' he said.

'So has meeting you, Jack.'

Molly bustled back into the room. 'Sorry to have left you alone so long,' she said. 'Have you two kept your-selves amused?'

'Oh, yes,' said Jack, with a wry smile.

Jack sat in his office and gazed out of the window. Winter was coming. The trees in the hospital grounds were bare of leaves, black branches a stark outline against a washed blue sky. He shivered and spun his chair round. Gloomily, he realised his room wasn't much more hospitable.

In most offices he visited there was some attempt at softening the harsh impression made by the basic hospital furniture. Other consultants tried to impress a little of their personality on their rooms. There were flowers or potplants, perhaps pictures on the wall, a set of family photographs.

Jack had none of these. For him his office was an extension of the hospital. There was a desk, kept as bare of papers as possible, bookcases and filing cabinets, two chairs drawn up opposite his desk. The only personal touch was the coffee-percolator in the corner.

The impersonality of the room was a deliberate decision. He hadn't wanted people in here thinking about him, wondering about who he was. He had wanted them solely to think of his work. Now he was wondering if that was a good idea.

Yesterday he had left the Landmoss clinic intending to think about Miranda Gale, to consider what he had half promised her. She had said he was detached and distant, had suggested that he try to be more…friendly? He hadn't told her that keeping his distance from people had at first been a deliberate decision, that had then changed into a habit. He didn't know how easy it would be to change back. He didn't know if he really wanted to.

But last night there had been a paper to write. This morning he had had a full list. He had had no time for anything but work. But now…just for a moment…he could think about her.

He thought he was too intelligent, too mature to be over-influenced by mere physical appearance. Even so, he had to admit that Miranda was absolutely gorgeous. Slightly taller than average, with a figure a little more full than was usual. Very different from the women he occasionally took out. A face to die for, with sparkling sapphire blue eyes that betrayed everything she was thinking. If Miranda was angry with you, there was no way she could hide it. Quite different from his own habit of keeping all feelings masked.

This was foolish! No time to sit here dreaming like an adolescent, he had work to do. But before he tore his thoughts away he remembered Miranda's lips. Too often he'd seen them tight with anger or frustration. And when she was puzzled, white teeth tended to bite the bottom lip.

They were lips he— What was he thinking of! Then, coolly and deliberately, he let himself think it. They were lips he would very much like to kiss.

Quite impossible, of course. She worked at the hospital. There was no way he'd ever get involved with someone from work again. He wasn't looking for a time-consuming affair either. And now he'd faced his feelings, acknowledged to himself how he felt, he could get on with his work. Keeping Miranda at a distance would hurt, of course. But he could stand pain.

He glanced at his watch. He had asked SHO Annie Arnold to come and speak to him. And, punctual to the minute, there was a knock on his door. 'Come in,' he called.

Annie entered. 'You wanted to see me, Jack?' She was obviously a little nervous, her green eyes apprehensive.

'I do. Annie, I arranged shift patterns for the SHOs before I went to America. When I'd gone you negotiated a change—you swapped a couple of daytime shifts for a couple of nights. Right?'

Annie coloured. 'It didn't seem to do any harm,' she said.

'Perhaps not. But because you didn't arrange things quite properly, two sets of patient notes went astray and I had to spend an hour yesterday chasing them.'

'I'm very sorry,' Annie said, now red-faced.

Jack looked at her. He liked Annie, thought she was a good SHO. And he remembered what he had promised Miranda.

'OK, it's not the end of the world,' he said gently. 'Let's remember that we're both doctors and that everyone makes mistakes sometimes. In the past I've swapped shifts so I could be with someone who I—'

'You have?' Annie asked incredulously.

'I have. Just not recently. Now, let me pour you a cup of coffee. I'll have one, too.'

She was obviously amazed at this small act of kindness and it hurt a little to see her amazement. Then he wondered if he would have felt like this before he had talked to Miranda.

He poured two coffees. Annie took hers, then dropped her spoon on the floor. 'Oh, what next?' she groaned as she leaned over and scrabbled under his desk.

Jack surprised her—and himself—by laughing. 'Leave it! Just so long as you don't go dropping scalpels inside patients. Now, while you're here, I may as well

go over your progress over the past couple of months.
I've been pleased with you. I think you have the
makings of a surgeon…'

It was an interesting few minutes he spent with her
and he found himself getting to know Annie the person
behind the very efficient doctor. Just before she left he
asked casually, 'Who was that nurse you brought into
Theatre the other day?'

'Miranda Gale? She's just started. In fact, we share a
flat together. Oh, Jack, she's so sorry that she fell and…'

He raised a hand. 'It doesn't matter. Just an accident.
The head of midwifery thinks very highly of her, feels
we are lucky to have her. But the beginning of November—it's an odd time to start work.'

'I think something happened to her some time ago
and she wanted to…' Annie started, and then obviously
decided to say no more. Instead she said, 'Look, it's not
for me to say…'

'That's understandable. Don't worry, Annie.'

Annie stood and moved towards the door. Then she
turned. 'Er, Jack. Could I ask you to do something for me?'

'I will if I can.'

Annie coloured again, very slightly. 'Don't say
anything to anyone about swapping shifts to anyone. I
organised it and now I want it forgotten.'

'OK, Annie, I'll say nothing. It's over and done with.'

Annie left and Jack thought about the meeting. He
had tried to be pleasant. He thought he had succeeded—
and he quite liked it.

Time to move over to Theatre and start scrubbing up.

But as he walked through the department he detoured a little to look in on the side ward where he knew Miranda was working. No special reason, he didn't intend to talk to her, just to look at her through the ward window.

She was on her own, a baby clasped in her arms. Her head was bent, she was smiling at the child, and her lips were moving. Like so many of the midwives, she talked to her charges. But she looked so happy, so at peace. He couldn't take his eyes off her.

He remembered how Annie had started to tell him about Miranda. She had said that something had happened to her…and then had stopped. Obviously a confidence. For a moment he wondered what Miranda's story was. Then he dragged his eyes away, pulled himself together and headed briskly to Theatre.

CHAPTER TWO

SHE hadn't intended to creep up on him. She was starting her shift and she found Jack alone in a side ward, holding one of the babies.

Perhaps he had just picked up little Scott to examine him. Scott's parents were coming in to take him home, perhaps he wanted to make one last inspection. But there was a real gentleness in the way that he was holding the baby, more emotion in his expression than Miranda had ever seen him show. Except when he had been playing a lion.

He looked up and saw Miranda. Instantly his features rearranged themselves and he was the cool, dispassionate surgeon again. 'Just making a last check,' he said, carefully placing little Scott back in his cot.

'There's no need to explain. I love holding babies, too,' she said. 'And though they're so young and so tiny, I know they can feel that love.'

'You think that love is some strange, intangible force that can pass from parent to child? Even a child as young as this?'

She realised his question wasn't trying to mock what she had said. He genuinely wanted an answer. 'I'm certain of it. Aren't you?'

'Well, there have been studies that suggest—'

'Forget studies! This is to do with how you feel, not how you think. Everyone's been so close to someone that they know they are loved. Haven't you?'

He didn't answer, and suddenly she realised just how personal her question was. 'Sorry,' she mumbled. 'That's not the kind of question I should ask.'

'Perhaps not, Miranda. But it's OK.'

She looked up, saw his smile and realised that he was teasing her. 'So do I get an answer, then?'

His smile disappeared. But there was sadness rather than anger in his face.

'I think I recognise the love you're talking about,' he said. 'Yes, perhaps I have felt it. A long time ago.'

Then his expression changed, became professional again. The slight intimacy between them was now over, they had work to do. 'I believe the parents are in the waiting room,' he said. 'Could you bring them through, please?'

'Of course.'

Sarah and Peter Downs had both been almost speechless at the knowledge that the child they had longed for was now going to live after all. It had been a hard birth, a baby with so many difficulties. And these had been remedied, repaired, by this man.

As she held Scott, Sarah was smiling, as if she'd been given something that she'd never believed she'd have. And—it was not at all unusual—her husband was in tears. Not taking her eyes off her son, Sarah said, 'You did this for us, Mr Sinclair. It was all down to you. You saved our baby's life.'

'Not at all. It was a comparatively simple operation and was entirely a team effort. Now, you've been given details of how to look after young Scott here. Don't be frightened by how small he is, he's going to grow. And if you ever have the slightest worry, phone here straight away. I wish you all the best—you've got a lovely little boy there.'

Jack shook hands with Sarah and Peter and left.

'I'll take you downstairs now.' Miranda smiled. 'It'll also give me a chance to say goodbye to Scott.'

Half an hour afterwards Miranda put her head round Jack's office door. 'The Downs have gone. They were so happy,' she said. 'When she held her baby she was crying with joy, and…she wanted to give you something. Something special.'

Then she caught herself. She'd been getting on with Jack quite well, they were getting to know each other—professionally, of course—perhaps even getting to like each other. She admired his surgeon's skill, felt he approved of her competence as a midwife and children's nurse. But as yet they were feeling each other out. No one could call them close friends. Though—surprisingly—she thought they might become friends.

'Something special?' he asked. 'A box of chocolates is fine but I don't really approve of gifts from parents to…'

Well, she was only passing on a message. 'Mrs Downs wanted to give you a big kiss. So she asked me to pass it on to you.'

Then she realised what she had said and went bright red. 'No! I don't mean that she wanted me to kiss you. I mean she wanted me to pass the message... Oh, no.' She winced. This was not the way to further her career in the Dell Owen Hospital. Perhaps he thought it was a come-on from her. And it wasn't. She did not, not, not want a relationship. Not for quite a while yet.

Afterwards, she realised that he had handled an embarrassing situation of her making well. He laughed and said, 'Well, whatever Mrs Downs wants, Mrs Downs should have. If you don't mind, that is.' And he offered her his cheek.

Her face flaming, Miranda kissed his cheek. Chastely. Well, what other way could you kiss a cheek?

But she enjoyed being close to him. She remembered how he had smelt when he'd come into the staff lounge at Landmoss, a mixture of expensive aftershave and body warmth. He smelt just like that now.

'But I think you probably shouldn't make a habit of passing on kisses for people. People might start to wonder.'

'Yes, they might. I think I'll go now.'

She wondered what her friends would say if she told them that she had just kissed the aloof Jack Sinclair. Then she thought of something else. He had asked—well, offered himself—to be kissed. He certainly hadn't had to. Was that usual?

* * *

Miranda met Annie for coffee again that lunchtime. They hadn't seen each other since the previous day.

'I went to see Jack yesterday, expecting a real telling-off,' Annie told her, shaking out her dark curls. 'And, in fact, I deserved it. But he was really nice. Got me to sit down, gave me a coffee, talked about my career. When you get underneath that cold exterior, he's quite pleasant. He asked about you.'

'Oh, yes? What did he want to know?' Miranda tried to speak carelessly, hoping her friend wouldn't notice her very real interest.

'Nothing much. Just a general enquiry. He thinks you're a good nurse.'

'I do my best,' Miranda said. But was that all he thought about her?

'He seems to have changed a bit,' Annie went on. 'Not the same cool man he was before. Perhaps he met someone in America, and she's having a softening influence on him.'

'It's a possibility,' Miranda agreed, then she firmly changed the subject.

After lunch she found some advertising brochures in the nurses' rest room. The hospital was regularly inundated with expensively printed advertising material. There were a couple of them that, just possibly, ought to be seen by a doctor. Perhaps she'd drop them into Jack's office. See what he thought.

'Come in, Miranda,' he said after she had hesitantly knocked. He smiled as she entered. 'If you're not in a hurry, would you like a coffee?'

'I would like a coffee but I am in a hurry. Unfortunately.' She placed the advertising material on his desk. 'I just wondered if these might be of any interest to you.'

She blushed slightly as she said this. She suspected that he knew it was just an excuse to come to see him.

'I'll look at them later. Have you time to sit down?'

In fact, she hadn't. In precisely five minutes she was due to relieve a midwife who had been on the morning shift and would be anxious to get home. 'No, I'm afraid not.' Then, daring, she added, 'But I'd like to some other time.'

This was the new Miranda Gale. She'd never have been so forward eighteen months ago.

But Jack didn't seem to mind. 'Good.' He looked at her and from his expression she couldn't work out exactly what he was feeling. Was he laughing at her? Did he want something from her? Was he just curious about her? Whatever, his expression now made her feel uncomfortable.

'You extracted a promise from me yesterday,' he said. 'And I always try to do what I have promised. So am I being more pleasant?'

'You've only been trying for two half-days but perhaps you're improving. And I think that people you work with are a bit more at ease. And our babies are just as well looked after.'

He growled. 'They'd better be. Any lowering of standards and I... Are you laughing at me?'

'I see the old Jack Sinclair hasn't disappeared yet,' she said.

'He might be less trouble than the new Jack Sinclair.

Tell me, Miranda, what do you know of the law of un-intended consequences?'

She frowned. 'The what?'

'The law of unintended consequences. It states that whenever you change something, no matter how good your intentions, there is a chance that something entirely unexpected will happen.'

'So?'

'So you want me to change. How do you think that will affect you personally? What consequences might there be for you?'

She was feeling flustered now. 'No consequences. Why should there be?'

'Who knows?'

He stared at her imperturbably and went on, 'And this morning you kissed me. And I liked it—and so did you. Could that have unforeseen consequences?'

'That was a kiss from Mrs Downs,' Miranda quavered, knowing this was one of the most stupid things she had ever said. 'It was only on the cheek.'

'Of course it was. There was absolutely no feeling for me on your part. Was there?' He looked at her, his face bland, enquiring.

'Well, not really, I... It was just a spur-of-the-moment thing... I just thought...'

She knew she was red-faced with embarrassment and when she looked up she saw he was smiling at her. He was teasing her! She wouldn't have too much of that. Not any more. So she said, 'Jack, it was only a kiss on the cheek. But, yes, I enjoyed it. Did you?'

Then her mouth dropped open and she gasped, 'Did I ask you that?'

'Only we two are in the room,' he said. 'You must have done.' He picked up the brochures she had brought in. 'Thanks for these. I'll look at them later.'

'And I've got work to do.' She was glad to escape. Only as she hurried down the corridor did she realise he hadn't answered her question. Had he enjoyed being kissed by her? She was being ridiculous.

Jack closed his eyes as Miranda left his office, letting the brochures fall on the papers he had been reading before she'd knocked on his door. Teasing aside, yes, he'd enjoyed that kiss, even if it had been only on the cheek. Enjoyed the brief closeness and warmth. The delicate scent of her as her lips had brushed his skin. Enjoyed it far too much.

Miranda Gale intrigued him, more than intrigued him. But it had been so long since he'd let someone get close to him. And not only that, she was a colleague. If people started to notice something between them, the hospital grapevine would go into overdrive.

He'd had enough of being talked about, gossiped about. That's why he kept himself to himself and his colleagues at arm's length. So why was he breaking his strict rule—did he want to risk being the talk of the hospital again? His aloof façade was there to protect him from all that. Work and pleasure he kept distinctly separate. Veronica had taught him that lesson.

Crossly, he shoved the magazines aside and tried to

concentrate on his papers. But despite his rigid control, the memory of Miranda's blue eyes closing as she'd reached up to him, her soft lips gently pressing to his skin, refused to go away.

Miranda worked happily for the next two hours. It was simple but absorbing work, specialling two babies who needed constant care. Connor Jones and Shannon Castle needed hourly obs, hourly feeds. She was see-sawing Connor's milk, gradually increasing the amount of milk and decreasing the glucose drip. She had to make sure he could tolerate the increased volume—but so far he was doing well and seemed to be enjoying the feeling of a full tummy for the first time. It made the job worthwhile.

Shannon had developed jaundice. She was under phototherapy lights to allow the lights to break down the bilirubin tingeing her skin yellow. Left unchecked, excess bilirubin could lead to brain damage.

And as Miranda worked she thought about Jack. There was a sense of possibilities, a wondering about the way he had looked at her. Now he knew she was a woman. She could tell by the way his eyes had hooded slightly, by the easy way he'd smiled. She wondered what he had meant when he had talked of the law of un-expected consequences. There was obviously an under-lying message for her. And the talk about kissing!

She had to be careful. Her life over the past few months had been full of hurt. And though there was something drawing her to Jack, she didn't want to risk that again. And she still felt that gaping sense of loss.

For a moment she busied herself with the baby in her care, tried to control the tears that were welling in her eyes. She was getting better! She was learning to cope, think about something else!

She did think about something else. And she realised that every time she saw Jack she was more aware of the lean body, the face she had called craggy. How anyone could call him ugly...

She had finished for the day and was alone in the sisters' room. She'd just finished handover, briefing the midwife who would take over from her. Now it was home and a well-deserved rest... The phone rang. Miranda sighed. You couldn't ignore a ringing telephone in an obs and gynae department.

'I want Jack Sinclair! Where is he? I want Jack Sinclair!'

The speaker sounded like a young girl. And she also sounded hysterical.

'I'm sorry, Mr Sinclair is operating,' Miranda said cautiously. 'There's absolutely no way he can be disturbed. I'm Miranda Gale, I'm a midwife here. Can I help you with anything? Or would you like to talk to someone else?'

'No, you can't help me. Nobody can help me, I want Jack Sinclair. I want him now!'

Miranda didn't like the note of desperation in the voice. 'I'm afraid that's quite impossible,' she said. 'He's in the middle of a long operation on a very sick baby. I just wouldn't dare to go and speak to him. But I will as soon as he finishes.'

That appeared to make some sense to the girl. 'Suppose another hour or two won't matter,' she mumbled. 'Things can't get any worse. Pills don't help and—'

'What pills?' Miranda was instantly alert.

'I said they don't help. Nothing helps, there's nobody can help. Just forget it. I—'

Miranda thought the girl was about to ring off, so she said urgently, 'I'm sorry, I didn't get your name. And the address is…?'

'I'm Danielle Benson. He knows my address.' And then there was the burr of the replaced receiver.

Miranda sighed. It wasn't unusual to get half-hysterical phone calls at the hospital. Jack presumably knew this girl so all she had to do was leave him a note for when he came out of the operating theatre. But Miranda wasn't going to do that. She'd wait and tell Jack in person. She wasn't quite sure why.

He looked tired when he came out of Theatre, sat slumped in his scrubs in the changing room, and the look he gave her was distinctly cool. But when he saw her expression, his demeanour changed. 'Miranda, you look serious,' he said. 'Have I done something wrong?'

She sat by him. 'Not quite,' she said. 'A girl—or a woman—phoned about an hour ago, demanding to talk to you. You alone, no one else would do. Then she rang off. Name was Danielle Benson. She mentioned pills.'

Jack sighed. 'It's not my case any more. Danielle had a baby with a pyloric stenosis. I operated on her and the baby survived. Apparently she's doing well. The baby was my responsibility for a month and then Paediatrics and Social Services took over. But for some reason Danielle fastened on me. Thought I'd saved the life of her baby so I could do everything for her. She's rung several times. I've reassured her and told her to get in touch with her social worker or her GP, but she refuses.'

Miranda frowned. 'So are you going to see her now?'

He looked unhappy. 'One of the biggest mistakes a doctor can make is getting involved with the personal lives of his patients.'

'I know that. But you are going to see her, aren't you? She sounded desperate.'

He shrugged. 'I'll phone her now and promise to call round later. There's not a lot I can do but I can be there.'

'Would you like me to come with you?'

Surprised, he looked at her. 'Is that an offer of help?'

'I used to be a district midwife in Leeds and I worked some of the hardest districts there. I'm used to hard cases.'

'Why should you want to come with me?'

'This problem should be something I'm good at. You're a surgeon, you've got vast scientific resources, dozens of willing helpers, your skills are concentrated on a tiny unconscious baby. But all that is exact. You forget, a lot of medicine is messier than surgery. People are more awkward than bodies. You should know that hospitals only solve about half of people's problems.'

He grinned at her. 'Well, that puts me in my place. Miranda, I'll accept your kind offer of assistance. I'll meet you in Reception in half an hour.'

Miranda hurried off, she didn't know what exactly she might need—if she would need anything—but she borrowed a district midwife's bag. It made her feel complete.

Then she wondered why she had volunteered to help Jack. She hadn't intended to do it when she'd passed on the message. But when she'd seen the black hair tumbling over his forehead, messed when he'd taken off his cap, and when she'd seen those tiny lines by his eyes and heard that deep voice, she'd wanted to spend time with him. No, she wanted to help him. She told herself firmly that that was all. And there was a baby who might need help.

Then she wondered if she was being wise. She couldn't afford to get…attached to Jack. Not that way. It would be a disaster for both of them. But an offer of help between friends was fine.

He had changed into a short coat, looked tougher than normal. Miranda had offered to drive, and as she drove, he told her about the case.

'Danielle Benson, aged twenty-one. Two kids, one boy Derek aged three, the second, Kylie, just a year old. I operated on Kylie. She seems to be doing well now.'

'Husband?'

'Wayne. He's been a waste of space, in and out of small-time trouble, in and out of prison. But I thought he was improving. The thing is, Danielle tries. She loves the kids to bits. She has a couple of cleaning jobs and all her money goes on the kids.'

'What pills was she talking about?'

Jack laughed, without much humour. 'As if she didn't

have enough to worry about. She's got high blood pressure, it rocketed after Kylie was born. She's on hypertensives and if she takes her medication she's all right.'

Miranda nodded. 'I know. And if she doesn't take the pills, she still feels fine. So why carry on taking them? And then, she doesn't know, but…'

'Possibly nothing. Or possibly a heart attack or a stroke. I see you've been there before.'

Danielle lived in a large multi-storey block of flats, not too far from the Landmoss clinic. A small figure in tight jeans and an extra-large sweater, she wrenched open the door the minute Jack tapped on it. 'Oh, Mr Sinclair. I'm so glad you've come! It's Wayne and he promised that he would…'

Jack eased her back into the living room. 'Good to see you, Danielle,' he said. 'Now, this is Miranda Gale, she's a midwife and a colleague of mine. The first thing we do is I want to have a look at you. Then you can make us some tea and we'll have a talk. Quietly and without getting excited.'

Miranda looked around. Danielle's living room was immaculate. The furniture was old but polished, there were photographs of the children on the walls and a few knick-knacks and ornaments were displayed on the mantelpiece and shelves. It was a pleasant room to be in.

'Have you been taking your pills?' Jack asked.

Danielle looked shamefaced. 'Missed them this morning,' she muttered. 'I was excited with Wayne coming out and all. But I took them later. It's all his fault he…'

'Sit over there and roll up your sleeve,' said Jack. 'I need to take your blood pressure, then listen to your heart. And you try to calm down. We can sort things out. Do you mind if Miranda here takes a look at the kids?'

'They're asleep. Derek's been that excited at seeing his dad and…'

Jack took her by the arm, led her to a chair. 'Sit down, close your eyes, take a couple of deep breaths. We can sort things out.'

He nodded to Miranda. 'First door on the left. They're lovely kids.'

They were. It was a tiny bedroom, but there were toys there, pictures of numbers on the wall and shelves filled with neatly folded clothes. Derek, the older, was firmly asleep, and one-year-old Kylie was just starting to grizzle. Miranda waited a moment, then picked the baby up. She was obviously not going to settle.

Back in the living room Miranda saw a side of Jack she'd not seen before. Previously she had thought him pleasant but aloof, keeping most people at a distance. Now she saw just how friendly and approachable he could be. Danielle was crying. And Jack was comforting her.

Miranda felt just a little embarrassed. She had offered to come to help Jack, and had hinted that she thought that he couldn't cope with life in the raw. Now she saw she was wrong. Jack knew exactly how to comfort and reassure Danielle.

Miranda sat quietly in a corner and cuddled Kylie. She liked having the child so close to her, feeling the warmth and smelling that unique baby smell while she listened to Danielle's tearful story.

'He came out of prison yesterday. He swore he wouldn't go back, said he didn't need to do drugs no more, he'd been on a programme. He'd get a job—if he could. And you know, Mr Sinclair, I've been working myself. I've been putting a bit aside every week, so we could have a good Christmas. And then this afternoon a couple of his old pals came round and he went out with them. And when he'd gone I looked in my drawer, where I keep my extra money. And he'd taken the lot.'

Jack looked thoughtful. 'I thought he was on the right path, Danielle,' he said. 'I'm surprised. I thought he might have changed at last.'

'Well, he hasn't!' A clearly angry Danielle tried to keep her voice low. 'He's as bad as he was before, only worse. Now I just want rid of him.'

Miranda had heard many stories like this before. Being a district midwife was not just about babies.

'I wonder if you ought to—' Jack started, when there was the sound of a key in the door. The door opened and in walked Wayne. He was a thin, red-haired man, looking very apprehensive. He looked more apprehensive still when he saw Jack. 'Oh. It's you, Mr Sinclair,' he said.

'Where's my money? I worked for that money to give us a Christmas, and you…' Danielle hurled herself across the room, to be caught expertly by Jack. 'Danielle! Sit down and listen!'

To Miranda's surprise, Danielle did as she was told.

'This is not my problem,' Jack said to Wayne. 'If you want, I'll go. But I have a medical responsibility to the children, and I shall have to report that I'm not very happy about things here. Now, I can tell you've had a drink, but I doubt you've been taking drugs.'

'I'm not doing drugs! I've been on a programme and I'm sticking to it!'

'So where is Danielle's money?'

Wayne slumped onto a chair. 'You don't know what it's like inside. I owed these people some money and they aren't people you cross. There was just enough to pay them off, so I did.'

'You paid them off in full?'

'In full. In fact, there's a bit left, a fiver.'

'A fiver!' Danielle screamed. 'There was over two hundred in that drawer that I've saved, and my week's housekeeping as well!'

Wayne looked hunted. 'I'll get it back to you. Somehow.'

'Somehow? You haven't even got a job. Who'll employ you?'

'I know someone who'll employ him,' said Jack. And there was silence in the room.

Jack took out one of his cards, wrote an address on the back of it and handed the card to Wayne. 'That's a firm on the Dock Road. Get there before eight tomorrow and ask for Mr Callow. He's an old friend of mine, I'll ring him tonight. He'll give you work. It'll be hard and the pay isn't much at first, but it's work.'

Miranda looked at Wayne, who seemed unable to believe his luck. 'Thanks,' he mumbled. 'Won't let you down, Mr Sinclair.'

'It wouldn't be me you were letting down. It'd be Danielle and the kids.'

Then Jack reached for his wallet, took out a bundle of notes. Miranda couldn't help it, 'Jack,' she muttered, 'I wonder if...'

But he looked at her, a hard, deliberate look, and she said nothing more. Here he was in charge and she realised that he knew what he was doing.

He said, 'This is a loan. Eighty pounds housekeeping for you, Danielle, twenty for you, Wayne, you'll need some money to travel. Pay me back, twenty pounds a week—OK?'

'We're not taking your money,' Danielle snapped. 'We don't need charity.'

'You don't need money, your children do! And you're not getting charity, you're getting a loan! Right?'

'Right,' muttered Danielle. 'And you can count on it, you'll get it back.'

'Then we'll be off. Miranda, perhaps Wayne would like to hold Kylie now.'

Rather reluctantly, Miranda handed the now sleeping baby over. Jack had a couple more words with Danielle and then they were gone.

As they made their way down the stairs, Miranda sighed. 'I was wrong,' she said. 'You didn't need me, you knew exactly what to say and what to do and you did it.'

'I was glad you were there. You holding the baby meant I could concentrate on Danielle. And you seemed very taken with young Kylie.'

'She's a lovely baby. Jack, you lent them money. And we were told to never never never lend money to patients. I wanted to say something but...I didn't.'

'I'm glad. I know it was a risk. But sometimes in life you've got to take a risk. And I think this one was worthwhile.'

They walked out of the entrance to the car. With a smile she asked, 'Surgeons take risks?'

'I said in life, not in surgery.' He glanced at his watch. 'Now, I'd like to say thank you in some way. Would you like to stop off somewhere and have a drink?'

She thought. Yes, she really, desperately would like to have a drink with Jack. She was getting to know him, she was getting to like him. Perhaps in time they could... But she'd made arrangements!

'Well, I really would,' she said. 'But I've already arranged to go out with Annie and the others from the department. Annie won't go until I'm home to go with her.' She looked at him, hoping he could see how hopeful she was. 'Jack, we're going to the Red Lion together. Why don't you come along, too?'

'Because of you I have changed a bit,' he said. 'But don't rush me.'

Fifteen minutes later she was in her bath. Annie had phoned her to say she was going to be late so there was no hurry. So Miranda lay in her bath and pondered.

She had to think about Jack. She had to think about what he was doing to her. She had come to the Dell Owen Hospital determined to start afresh, to throw herself into both the professional and the social life. Well, she was loving the work. But the social life?

No need for false modesty, she knew she was attractive. So far, two men had invited her out. Nothing too exciting—one had invited her for a drink at the Red Lion, the other had asked if she'd like to go to a party with him. One was a SHO, the other a nurse. They had been friendly, casual invitations and she had quite liked both men. If she had accepted either invitation perhaps something might have come of it.

But, although she wanted to be part of the hospital social life, she hadn't accepted. And the reason was Jack. The two young men were fine. But compared with Jack, they were children. She had to admit it. She was attracted to Jack—but slightly frightened as well. Could she cope with his intensity?

Then she laughed ruefully to herself. Why worry if she could cope? So far he had been friendly but had shown no great indication that he was really interested in her. Or had he?

Miranda didn't know what to expect when she was summoned to his room two days later. Just a note in her pigeonhole—could she call in to see him when it was convenient?

He was sitting there in his usual dark suit and white shirt. She realised it was his uniform. Other doctors might have coloured shirts, bright ties. But Jack Sinclair would hide behind formality.

'I gather that on Saturday you're going to a conference in Leeds,' he told her, 'on Problems with TPN.'

TPN was total parenteral nutrition. Occasionally, often after surgery, an infant would be unable to take in sufficient nutrition by mouth. The answer was to feed the child through a catheter that led straight into a vein. There could be problems, often to do with nursing care. There was a risk of blood-borne infections because there was a direct opening into the bloodstream. And there could be problems with the solution that was being fed into the vein.

'That's right,' she said, slightly surprised. 'How did you know?'

'I'm going myself and I got the attendance list this morning. You know there are some separate sessions, one for nurses and the other for doctors?'

'I know. I'm looking forward to learning something.'

'Good. So am I. How are you going to get to Leeds?'

'I'll take my battered old car. It'll get me there.' She grinned. 'Why? Do you want a lift?'

'Actually, I wondered if *you* would like a lift. I'm driving up, too, and it seems foolish to take two cars.'

'Yes, I would like a lift,' she said after a moment's thought. 'Thank you very much.'

'I'll enjoy taking you. Now, I'll pick you up at eight. Where do you live?'

Why did she feel so elated when she left his room? It was only a colleague being helpful to another. Wasn't it?

* * *

Jack stared at the door that Miranda had just closed and wondered what he had just done. It had not been a sudden decision, he had thought about it all the previous night. So much so that in the end he had got angry with himself. Why worry so much? This was only offering a colleague a lift to a conference. Nothing more than that.

But Jack had never deceived himself. When she had said she would come with him he had felt a sudden rush of pleasure, far more than was justified by a colleague just accepting a lift. He had also seen the spark of excitement in her eyes when she said she'd come.

He had told her when they left Danielle Benson's flat that sometimes people had to take a risk. Now he was taking a risk. For a long time now—perhaps too long—he had been the cool one, carefully detached from any kind of emotional life. Was he about to change? He didn't know.

Then he realised he was thinking just about himself. What about Miranda? All he could tell himself was that she attracted him more than any woman had done in years.

'He's giving you a lift to a conference?' Annie looked at her friend in amazement. 'To the best of my knowledge, he's never taken anyone anywhere before.'

'He said it was foolish to take two cars. Perhaps he's concerned about the environment.'

'Environment? That's a new name for it. He's giving you a lift because he fancies you. And because you're the best-looking woman in the department.'

'That's a nice thing to hear,' Miranda said, rather pleased with the compliment, 'but I don't think our surgeon is over-concerned with looks. He's far too serious.'

'Perhaps you're right.' Annie took Miranda's hands in her own, squeezed them a moment and then let go. 'One thing to remember, though—when you're a surgeon you have to have absolute confidence in yourself. I've watched him working, there's an intensity, a concentration to him that's almost frightening. Whatever he does, he does to the limit. And I suspect that'll include falling in love.'

'Annie! I'm going to a medical conference with him and there'll be a hundred other delegates there! This is not a day for romance.' Miranda wondered if she sounded sufficiently convincing.

'Perhaps that's not your intention—or his. But things can change very rapidly. Just how attracted to him are you?'

This was a question that had been occupying Miranda's mind. 'I'm still recovering from one disastrous love affair,' she said slowly, 'and I'll have to live with the consequences of that for the rest of my life. But Jack…he wakes feelings in me that I thought were dead. And perhaps they were better that way.'

Annie rose and hugged her friend. 'Good luck,' she said. 'You'll need it.'

What to wear when you're going to a medical conference with your consultant? Formal or festive? Bright coloured or sombre? Difficult choices. Annie helped her.

She was dressed and waiting for him at half past seven next morning. He arrived, as she'd guessed he would, precisely at eight. In his sleek black sports car. It matched his suit.

She was wearing a burgundy-coloured dress with a short suede jacket. She felt smart but professional. She wasn't expecting him to comment. But when he saw her he said, 'Miranda, you look good in scrubs or uniform. In a dress you look gorgeous.'

She looked at him in genuine surprise. 'Well thank you, kind sir. I didn't know you did compliments.'

'One of my less well-known skills. Shall we go?'

He drove with the same skill as he operated— precisely, expertly, safely. They quickly negotiated the suburbs and headed along the motorway towards Leeds. Miranda had never been driven in such a luxurious car before, and rather liked it. And she liked the feeling of confidence that Jack gave her. She knew she was safe with him. Well, safe from a road accident.

Miranda found the conference hard work, but she liked it. With TPN, first there was the danger of sepsis, of infection getting straight into the bloodstream. This was of particular interest to nurses, since they were in charge of the day-to-day welfare of their charges. The second danger was more subtle. No parenteral food could offer the complete nutrition that the baby needed. And sometimes the baby's immune system would reject the injected fluids. To combat this, an amino acid called glutamine could be used, which suppressed the immune system. But then there were other undesirable side effects.

The first couple of hours were joint sessions, for both

doctors and nurses, and Miranda found some of the scientific concepts were new to her. But after a break they split and she found the practical sessions for nurses to be very useful. She learned a lot, knew that in future she'd be a better children's nurse.

Jack enjoyed the conference, enjoyed being with Miranda. He too had learned quite a bit. But there was no doubt that her presence had made a reasonable day into a very good one. He thought she had enjoyed it, too, and was as sorry as she was when the conference ended.

They started for home. He liked driving, liked the feeling of being in control of the powerful car. And it was uncanny, Miranda guessed what he was thinking. 'A bit different from my antique rustbucket, isn't it?' she asked.

They felt the same things at the same time. He remembered what she had said about love when they had been in the little side ward. That it could be felt, recognised, without there needing to be anyone speaking. Not quite the same thing. But…the two of them seemed to get on so well.

He hadn't intended to do it, the decision was a sudden one. Just when they were at the top of the Pennines he turned off the motorway onto a side road. Suddenly they were away from the bright motorway lights and into the darkness of the moors. Then they turned off the side road onto something that was little more than a track.

Miranda was curious. 'Where are we going?' she asked.

'Just a little diversion, we'll only be fifteen minutes or so. Something I want to show you.' They stopped and he went on, 'Only a few yards walk from here. I...I often come here when I'm passing at night.'

'On your own?'

Now, that was an interesting question and it raised other questions but he avoided thinking about them. 'I very seldom have anyone with me when I come this way.'

He was still not quite sure why he had brought Miranda there.

He locked the car and side by side they walked up the track. At times their hands brushed, but he didn't reach out to take hers. Perhaps he would on the way back, he thought. Perhaps things would be different between them then.

It was dark, but there was a glow coming from the ridge just ahead of them. They reached the top of the path and he heard Miranda gasp.

Below them the ground fell away steeply. And as far as their eyes could see there were lights. A great golden pattern showing all the towns of Lancashire. It was wonderful.

'Why did you bring me here?' she asked.

He shrugged. 'It's beautiful, I love it and I thought you might, too.'

'I do find it beautiful,' she said.

'When you're operating your entire mind is focussed on one tiny subject. Important, but tiny. Every now and again I like to see things from a different perspective. And views like this help.'

They stood there side by side in silence, looking at

the view, hearing distant noises from the innumerable lives below them. Occasionally their shoulders touched.

Jack was indecisive, this was something he wasn't used to. Usually he knew what he wanted, went straight for it. But now he had the feeling that what he did in the next couple of minutes might have unforeseeable consequences. He realised his heart was beating faster. Him, the ice-cool surgeon Jack Sinclair!

He put his arm round Miranda's shoulders, pulled her towards him. He took her two hands in his spare hand. 'You haven't got a coat or gloves, you must be cold,' he said.

Both of them knew that this was an excuse to touch, to hold her. What would happen next?

She had kissed him. On the cheek and, all right, it had been a joke. Well, they had both treated it as a joke. But he wondered if she had felt the same as he had. That it would have been much more exciting if she had kissed him on the lips.

Should he kiss her now? He thought she'd like it, suspected she wanted to be kissed. But he also knew that one kiss would start an entirely new relationship between them. And the thought both worried and excited him. All the rules he had been living his life by broken. But with Miranda, he couldn't help himself...

'Don't lag behind at the back, Barry! Keep up with the others.'

What? *What?* He turned and sighed. Coming rapidly towards them was a neat crocodile of Cub Scouts. There was the sergeant-majorish figure of a leader in front. He gave a brisk 'good evening' to Miranda and Jack, and then said, 'Now, listen up! I want you to remember the constellations we discussed. Who can tell me where…?'

Jack could hear the giggle in Miranda's voice as she whispered, 'I don't think he's too happy at sharing his astronomy lesson with a couple holding hands. Perhaps we ought to go.'

'It might be a good idea.'

He did hold her hand as they walked down the path. That was something. But he had a feeling that a decision had been avoided.

Miranda also knew that something had been postponed. But what happened next would have to be Jack's decision. She would wait. She hoped she didn't have to wait too long. How she would deal with things was a different matter.

The rest of the trip back was relaxed and pleasant. They listened to music on his very expensive stereo system—both had similar tastes. They chatted casually about the possibility of introducing a research programme on the use of glutamine in the department. And all too soon they pulled up outside her flat.

It wasn't late, just before eight o'clock. Miranda didn't want to get out of the car. 'I've enjoyed today,' she said. 'Thank you for taking me, Jack.'

He seemed in no hurry for her to go. 'I've enjoyed being with you, too. What's your programme for tonight? Out on the town?'

'I've had enough excitement for one day and it's

been a hard week. Probably tea and then a couple of hours in front of the TV. What about you?'

'I'm on call from ten o'clock onwards. I'll get something to eat at the hospital and then sleep there the night. It's not very likely that I'll be wanted, but I've got to be available.'

Still no movement from either of them. And the silence between them was comfortable. As she went back over her day with him, it struck her that she couldn't remember the last time she'd enjoyed herself so much with a man. Beneath that apparently cool exterior there was a man who was generous, witty, fun to be with. The word *passionate* came into her mind but she shied away from it; she didn't want to think about Jack and passion.

It came as a shock. She realised that she could very easily fall in love with Jack. So far in her life, love hadn't been too good for her, she had to be cautious. To fall in love with Jack could be bad, to have Jack fall in love with her could be a disaster for both of them. She thought that he was a man whose emotions, once stirred, might be hard to control. She didn't want to bring that misery to him. Or to herself.

She felt him turning to face her. She knew he would escort her to the front door of her flat, but before that, would he just say goodnight? Would he kiss her? If he kissed her, would it be just a friendly kiss on the cheek or forehead, a chaste kiss on the lips or…? She remembered the last time she had kissed him. A joking friendly kiss on the cheek. But how she remembered it. And now she didn't want him to go.

It happened almost without thinking. 'Would you like to come into the flat and have tea with me?' she asked. 'You're within easy reach of the hospital if you're needed.'

Obviously he hadn't expected this. 'Tea with you?'

'Yes. It'll only be shepherd's pie but it'll be good, it's my signature dish. I make it in large quantities and freeze it. What makes it so good is that I grate cheese on top of it and grill it.'

With dismay she realised that she was babbling. And she couldn't stop. 'You know I share the flat with Annie Arnold, don't you?'

She felt him tense a little. 'I'd forgotten that. It's just that you both work at the hospital and...'

'Don't you ever socialise with the staff? I've been to a couple of good nights at the hospital social club, been to the Red Lion once or twice. I've enjoyed myself. Why do you keep yourself so distant? You don't have to, you know.'

He leaned back in his seat again, apparently happy to sit there a little longer, to chat with her. 'You have an ability to ask personal and awkward questions,' he said. 'And, mysteriously, I find myself willing to answer them. One reason I try not to mix with the staff too much is that a few years ago I had an...entanglement with someone I worked with. It finished up all very messily, very emotional and my work suffered.' He thought a moment and then said, 'And so did I.'

'I'm sorry to hear that,' said Miranda, hating to think of Jack suffering, 'but thank you for confiding in me. Now do you want to come inside to eat shepherd's pie and risk being tangled again?'

She tried not to reveal her anxiety as she waited for his answer.

Eventually, 'I'd love to. And I don't tangle easily. Not now. In fact I never did.'

The lights in the road shone on his face and she could see he was smiling. Greatly daring, she said, 'When you smile your face is lovely.'

'Lovely?'

'Lovely,' she confirmed. 'You look like a friend I could tell anything to.'

'No one has ever said that to me before. Now lead on to the shepherd's pie.'

Well, Miranda reasoned, he wouldn't kiss her if they were going upstairs for tea.

CHAPTER THREE

MIRANDA hadn't been thinking. Perhaps she should have phoned her friend to warn her that their boss was coming to tea. As it was, she walked into the living room shouting, 'Hi. I'm home. Hope you don't mind but I've brought someone in for tea and—'

There was Annie, fresh out of the shower, still wet, with a towel wrapped round her dark hair and another one knotted precariously round her body. 'Oops,' Miranda said.

'Oops indeed,' muttered Annie as she saw Jack and scurried out of the room. A moment later she scurried back in and grabbed a handful of underwear that was drying in front of the fire.

With a grin Miranda looked at Jack and said, 'It's a risk you take when you mix with the staff at home. You might have to see their bright red knickers.'

'It's a risk I'll take,' he said dryly. 'I hope Annie isn't too uncomfortable with me being here.'

With a glint in her eye Miranda said, 'She'll get over it—Jack.'

Jack sighed. 'My life was much more peaceful before I met you,' he said.

'Perhaps you needed stirring up.'

It wasn't too long before the three of them were sitting at the little dining table. Annie had taken off the towels and was now in a safely long dressing-gown, her dark curls damp. The shepherd's pie was a distinct success, Miranda thought, and the accompanying vegetables weren't at all bad. 'Would you like a glass of red wine?' she asked Jack.

'I might have to work tonight. So just the one glass, please.'

'Just one glass is all you can have. There's only half a bottle left.'

He looked upset, made as if to stand. 'I'm so sorry. I'll fetch a couple of bottles from the—'

'Sit down and eat,' said Miranda. 'We don't need more wine.'

At first the conversation was a bit stilted. Miranda started by telling Annie something of the conference. Annie was obviously happier talking about something that was professional. But Miranda soon grew tired of it. There'd been enough lessons today!

'So where are you going tonight?' she asked Annie. 'Why that fancy dress laid out on your bed? Anyone nice?'

'Not anyone special, just a lot of old friends. It's a reunion dinner for my old hockey club. I used to play a lot—in fact, I was a county player. I rather miss it.'

Jack was interested in this. 'You used to be a county-class hockey player? Why did you give it up? Not an injury?'

Annie laughed. 'What happened was I became a SHO. And when I started, this man talked to us and said that for the next two years or so being a SHO was all our life. There would be time for little else.'

Jack looked at her and said mildly, 'I didn't know you were a county-class hockey player, did I? We might be able to arrange—'

'No,' said Annie. 'I didn't think so at the time, but now I know you were right. Being a SHO is a full-time job and more. You were right to tell me. And I'll still be young enough to play when I'm through it.'

Jack smiled his wry smile. 'I wish all my SHOs had your sense,' he said.

Miranda thought the meal went well. Jack was complimentary about her shepherd's pie, and she was sure that he meant it and was not being merely polite. Afterwards they sat on the couch and had coffee, then Annie excused herself and went to get changed. Jack rose to his feet. 'Perhaps I ought to go now, too,' he said.

Miranda couldn't look at him, he might guess what she was feeling if he saw her face. Her heart was beating far faster than it should but somehow she managed to keep her voice casual. 'No need to rush off,' she said, 'if you're only going to hang about at the hospital. Stay here and watch television with me for a while.'

'Would you mind?'

'Not at all. I'd welcome the company. If you want, we can—'

Annie came into the room, now in her party dress. 'You look lovely,' Miranda cried and added, forgetting herself, 'Doesn't she, Jack?'

'Very nice indeed,' Jack said urbanely. 'Annie, that is a definite improvement on scrubs.'

'Thank you both. Now, that sounds like my taxi outside. Er…hope you can come again, Jack.' She went to the door, where she turned, looked pointedly at Jack and then at Miranda. Miranda had difficulty stopping herself laughing. She had never seen so many conflicting emotions in a face. There was shock, excitement and a definite warning. Miranda should be careful. Then she was gone.

'I'm going to change out of these clothes,' Miranda said. 'I've been formal long enough. Why don't you take off your jacket and tie?'

'Thanks, I'd like that.'

'While I'm gone you can either look for something on the box or you can run though our collection of CDs. And pour yourself another coffee.'

She changed quickly, into a loose shirt and jeans. She'd worn tights for long enough, she decided, and went barefoot—more comfortable.

She knew she was making a decision. Hours earlier, when they had been alone on the moors looking down at the lights below, she had felt him tensing, and knew what he wanted to do. What she had wanted him to do. Now perhaps they could start again.

She sat by him on the couch. Nothing was said; they both listened to gentle music. Then he put his arm round her shoulders. Just for a moment she hesitated, felt her body stiffen. Then she relaxed and leaned against him. Where this would go she had no idea, but it felt good and right. And she wanted it. If only for a while.

For a while she sat there, quite comfortable, with his arm holding her against him and her arm round his waist. She was conscious of his body, could feel the warmth of his skin under her arm, could smell the faint citrus blend of aftershave he used. There was the rise and fall of his chest, a faint but exciting pleasure as he wrapped his fingers in her hair, stroked the back of her neck.

Then he kissed her. She had been expecting his kiss, hoping for it, even fearing it. But when it came it was pure delight. Now she knew that this was what she had been wanting. His lips on hers were hesitant at first, teasing, tantalising, making her need and want more. Then he kissed her cheeks, her half-closed eyes, her forehead. He bent his head to the side of hers and took the most delicate part of her ear into his mouth. She felt his teeth and shuddered with delight. Did he know just what effect he was having on her? Her body felt liquid, as if she had no control over it. Because she was with him!

Then he took her mouth again and his kiss became more insistent, demanding. His arms pulled her to him she gasped at the strength, the firmness of his body. She was aware of feelings stirring inside her that had been dormant for months—years even. There was a need, a desperation, a wild desire to give herself to this man. But with that need came a jarring note of caution. This wasn't really right.

He was sensitive, and felt her doubts, Slowly, reluctantly he stopped kissing her. But he held her still and they gazed at each other. In his dark grey eyes she saw a tenderness that had never been there before. The cool, hard man had disappeared. This was someone who desperately wanted to give. And wanted someone to give to. And that couldn't be her.

'We must stop,' she said. 'I don't think I'm good for you.'

A finger traced down the side of her face. 'I think you're very good for me,' he said. 'You make me feel happy and wanted and…needed.'

'You mustn't say that!' She moved away from him, took his arm from her shoulders. Then she decided that this was going too far, so she leaned forward and took his two hands in hers.

'Jack, you're a serious man. I suspect that if you're in a relationship you want it to have meaning.'

'Not always, Miranda. And who knows what the future might bring? But I think that a relationship with you might become serious.'

'It mustn't, it can't! Just now—I know I led you on and perhaps I shouldn't have. But I'm just a good-time girl. Frivolous, really.'

'You are not a good-time girl,' he said. 'That I do know. I have some knowledge of people. And when we're together, it all seems very right. As if we belong.'

'I'm not good for you!'

She saw his expression darken, the old, cold personality taking over. 'That, of course, is your decision to make.

I'm very sorry. I shouldn't have…have made advances to someone I work with. It's unprofessional and—'

'Jack, that's rubbish and you know it! You're not to hide your feelings behind what you think is proper.' She leaned over, quickly kissed him. 'And, besides, I can look after myself. It's just that I think that we two are…well, we need to get to know each other.'

She could see him thinking. His shoulders were hunched, there were lines on his forehead. And then she felt his body relax. 'So we do,' he said. 'Annie once let something slip, though she covered up quickly. She said something happened to you in the past. And, whatever that was, I think it affected you more than you know.'

'Oh, I know how it affected me,' she said bitterly. 'How well I know.'

He reached for her, eased her downwards until she lay with her head in his lap. She put her arms around his waist, lifted her legs onto the couch. This was so comforting!

'For the moment, things are fine as they are,' he said. 'We'll just get to know each other. You can forget your worries over your past and I'll try to forget that I'm a man with a poker for a backbone. We'll take things easy—and that for me is a first.'

He wriggled, kissed her lightly and made her more comfortable, leaning against his chest. 'There's so much I want to know about you, Miranda. I've no idea of your background, so tell me. What about your family?'

'My family? Hmm. They're all in New Zealand. My older brother emigrated first, and got married out there. Then my parents went out to visit him. Liked it so much that they decided to stay. We keep in touch but I've never quite managed to get out there to see them.'

'Why hasn't a gorgeous girl like you been snapped up by someone?'

She frowned. 'Well, I was engaged. Sort of. The something that happened to me was a car crash. I was injured, but the man with me was killed.'

'A car crash! I'm so sorry to hear that, sorry about your fiancé. Were you badly injured?' He sounded alarmed.

She didn't want to go into too much detail about the crash, not yet anyway. And Jack didn't notice her slight hesitation. 'I was injured but I recovered. But I was changed as well. In fact, I changed myself deliberately.'

She didn't want to move away from him but it would only be for a minute. She went to her bedroom, returned with a picture and snuggled back down next to him. 'This is the me as I used to be.'

He looked at the picture she had handed him and frowned. 'But you look older here. Look at the length of your hair. I like it better now it's short. And you're wearing glasses.'

'I had a haircut, got a new style and colouring. And I'm still having difficulty with my contact lenses. But I'll improve.'

'And where are those gorgeous legs? This skirt is far too long.'

'I ditched the skirt. I ditched most of my clothes.'

He was nodding as if he understood. 'After the crash you re-invented yourself, didn't you? Decided to become a new, different Miranda.'

'That's right. I nearly died. And when I didn't die, I asked myself if I wanted to look and act as I was doing for the rest of my life. And I decided I didn't. I became a new Miranda.'

'And who was this man you were sort of engaged to?'

'Ken Lassiter, a doctor at my hospital. He was outgoing, noisy, the life and soul of every party. He was always in charge. My job was to be silent and admiring. I was looking forward to marriage and children, while he was in no great hurry.'

She wiped a tear from her face, toughened up her voice. 'I knew he was drunk when we got into the car but I didn't object too hard, that wasn't my job. But sometimes I still wonder if somehow I killed him. A girl who was tougher would have refused to let him drive. But, as ever, I went along with things. After the crash I got lots of money in compensation. But it's never enough! And when I came round in hospital I vowed that never again would I be subservient to a man. I'd change my appearance, become a different person. And coming here, coming to a large city, that was going to be part of the change.'

He kissed her again. 'I like the new you,' he said.

Of course, there was more to her accident, but she didn't want to tell him now. She just couldn't—though she knew she was storing up trouble.

He must have realised that she didn't want to talk any more for a while. He hugged her, held her close to him and she felt that she was blissfully happy just lying there. But after a while it struck her that the conversation had been a bit one-sided.

'You know about me—what about you?' she asked. 'Why haven't you been snapped up? You told me earlier that you had been...entangled and you didn't like it.' Then she giggled, 'Look at the way I'm lying here now. I'm entangled with you.'

'In a much nicer way. You know I'm kept very busy. But there have been girlfriends from time to time.'

'The hospital gossip is that you go out with glamorous women who like appearing in the papers.'

He sighed. 'I'm afraid there's a bit of truth in that. But I just go out with them. At the time we both know there's nothing serious in the affair.'

Miranda wriggled, felt the warmth of his body against her face. 'I'm not glamorous. Is your taste changing?'

'Apparently. Miranda, work keeps me busier than any man ought to be. I don't seem to have much time for a social life or even to think about the future. But if I did, I imagine it would include someone like you.'

'Jack! For now we're just getting to know each other. No long-range plans...'

'I didn't say planning,' he pointed out. 'I said imagining.'

'Very true.' She pulled herself closer to him, felt the muscles of his arms about her, smelt the cleanness of his shirt. 'You know what?' she mumbled. 'I've had a lovely day. But it came after a hard week and because I'm warm and comfortable and happy, I'm almost falling asleep. But tell me more about your future. What do you want to achieve? What do you want most in the world?'

For a moment he was silent, lost in thoughts that, to Miranda, seemed rather sad.

'Like you wanted, marriage and children,' he said quietly. 'Ideally four kids, but who knows?'

Miranda tensed, then forced herself to relax. She should have expected something like that. She knew how much he loved children.

'Four's rather a lot,' she managed to murmur. 'Settle for three?'

'If I had to.'

She yawned, pushed herself upright. 'Jack, you don't know how much I've enjoyed being with you this evening,' she said. 'But now I'm too tired to even think. And I'm not going to fall asleep on your lap.'

He kissed her yet again, stood himself. 'I'd better go,' he said. 'It's not likely that I'll be called out—but just in case, I'll get some sleep. Miranda, I've enjoyed today more than any day I can remember. I'll look back on it and think of it as a beginning.'

Somehow she could smile. 'I think we started before today,' she said.

As Jack drove home, he thought about Miranda and everything she'd told him. She was amazing to have coped with so much tragedy in her life. She was so strong, yet so vulnerable, too. He found himself aching to heal her pain, make her happy.

'Coming from you, that's rich,' he murmured. Had he ever made anyone happy? His patients, yes, the families of babies he had successfully operated on, yes. His mother, brother and sister—they loved him as much as he loved them. But anyone else? Certainly not Veronica.

Miranda made him happy. When he was with her, she made him forget about the past, forget that he believed he'd never trust again, never love again. With her, he finally felt he had hope for the future.

Miranda liked working with Jack's sister and she remembered how Annie had told her that the three Sinclairs were called the good, the bad and the ugly. Miranda had already decided quite definitely that Jack wasn't ugly. She had only seen Toby from a distance, but he seemed to be cheerful, happy, smiling, a fantastic doctor. He wasn't really bad, he wasn't a womaniser, he wasn't a serial seducer. He had a gift—or a curse. Every woman he smiled at seemed to fall for him.

And now Miranda could see why Carly—Toby's twin, Jack's sister—was called the good. She was soft-voiced, gentle, totally unlike her two brothers. There was a physical resemblance—they all had the large grey eyes, dark hair, were tall and long-legged. Miranda had liked her at once.

They were working together in the postnatal clinic, checking over the mums and new babies, making sure that all was well. Usually it was happy, enjoyable work.

It was three days after her trip to the conference, after Jack had stayed to tea and they'd had their talk. The Sunday following the talk he had phoned her. He had been called into hospital for an emergency case that would take quite a while to deal with. But he had been thinking of her.

'I've been thinking of you, too,' she had said. 'I'm wondering if I ought to apologise for dumping my troubles on you. Telling you about my accident,' she had added hastily.

'Friends are for dumping on, Miranda. I would have been angry if you hadn't told me.'

'Are you my friend?'

'I want to be your friend and I'd like to be more. But at the moment I'm a bit confused.'

She had listened to his voice, trying to analyse it. He certainly hadn't been the cool, dispassionate surgeon any more, there had been warmth in his tones.

They had chatted for a couple for minutes but she was glad when the call had ended. She didn't know where they were going—but they seemed to be going somewhere.

And now she was working with his sister.

'I'm glad to meet you,' Carly said when they had a minute's respite. 'I gather you've been out with my stern big brother, Jack. It's about time he met someone like you.'

'We didn't really go out together,' Miranda explained. 'Just to a conference. And he stayed for tea afterwards.'

'I know, Annie told me. But I saw him when he came out of Theatre on Sunday and he was smiling. He said he'd had a great time at the conference. And that must have been you. Now, what's this next case?'

This was to be the last check carried out by the hospital and was quite a detailed one. After this, if all was well, care of the mother and baby was handed over to the GP and the local health visitor.

'Name is Sophie Vesey,' said Miranda, handing over

the notes. 'There doesn't seem to be anything seriously wrong with her. I'll get her in if you want to look through these.' She went into the waiting room.

Other mothers and babies had formed little groups, were chatting among themselves, comparing notes. Sophie sat by herself, rocking the baby in her pram with one hand, a glossy magazine held in the other.

'Morning, good morning.' Sophie smiled at them as Miranda ushered her into the consultancy room. 'I gather this is the last time we'll meet.'

'Well, I hope so,' said Carly, and the three of them laughed.

Sophie was slim, appeared confident. She was older than average for a primigravida but had obviously decided that having a baby was no excuse for letting standards slip. She was modishly made up, with bright red lipstick. Her hair had been recently styled, her clothes recently bought. However, there was something about her that made Miranda vaguely apprehensive. But she couldn't quite decide what.

This was an interview that was best taken slowly. Carly started by chatting generally about how Sophie felt, what problems there had been. 'No problems at all,' Sophie said brightly. 'People warned me about how hard this would be. And I've had no trouble whatsoever. And baby Harry here is a darling.'

Both Carly and Miranda were surprised at this cheerfulness.

'You're getting enough sleep?' Miranda asked. 'A lot of new mums feel tired all the time.'

'I cope. I just don't seem to need so much sleep as I did.'

Now, that was unusual.

Miranda checked baby Harry first, he was in great shape. Then she helped Sophie get undressed and there was the normal examination. All seemed well. Then there was the internal, to check the cervix, the uterus, the pelvic floor. All fine there, too. And through all of this, Sophie kept up a good-humoured conversation, telling them how happy she was.

'You can get dressed now,' Carly said eventually. 'You seem in fine shape. Er…Sophie. You don't have to talk about this if you don't want to, but have you started having sexual relations with your husband yet? Is all well there?'

'No problems whatsoever. If anything, things are better than they were.'

'Well, you seem to have had a perfect pregnancy,' Carly said. 'I don't think we need to see you again.'

'There's the Edinburgh scale,' Miranda said. 'If Sophie wouldn't mind filling it in, it would give us some idea of just how good a perfect pregnancy can be. A sort of control.' She glanced at Carly, who nodded for her to continue. After all, Miranda had seen more pregnant women than Carly had.

'The Edinburgh postnatal depression scale,' Miranda explained to Sophie. 'You fill in answers to ten questions—just about how you are feeling. Obviously, it's not necessary in your case but we like to see healthy women as well as those who have problems. Why don't you take it outside and fill it in at your leisure?'

Sophie laughed. 'I'm going to get full marks, you know,' she said. 'But I'll do it.' She took the form Miranda handed her, bent down to kiss her baby and wheeled the pram out of the room.

There was a moment of silence. Then Carly asked, 'Miranda, have I missed something? I've never seen a more cheerful mother.'

'Neither have I,' said Miranda. 'But there's something wrong. She's too good to be true. Carly, I hope you don't mind, but could we have another doctor in? Just for five minutes?'

'I'll fetch Jack,' said Carly. 'I know he's in his room.'

'Jack? But he's a surgeon.' Miranda hadn't expected this.

'Jack knows a lot more about people than he lets on. Don't let him fool you.'

He doesn't need to fool me, Miranda thought, I think I'm fooling myself. But he might be able to help Sophie.

He came into the room with his sister. As usual, when she saw him for the first time, her heart gave a little thump. But this was just because he looked so gorgeous, she told herself. Just a reaction to his masculinity. Purely hormonal, nothing to do with feelings.

'Carly tell me that we've got the perfect post-partum mum,' he said with a smile. 'And you're not happy with her?'

'You know, I'm beginning to agree with Miranda,' Carly said thoughtfully. 'She is too perfect. It just isn't normal.'

'So this is a test. What explanations could there be?'

Then it suddenly came to Miranda. She blurted out, 'I've just remembered, I heard her talking and I know what her husband does. He's a dispensing chemist.'

The examination room suddenly seemed cooler. Not one of the three spoke for a moment and then Carly said, 'With access to all sorts of drugs.'

'I'll go and fetch her in, shall I?' suggested Miranda. 'See if she's finished the test.'

'Good idea,' said Jack. 'Carly, do you mind if I do the talking for a while?'

'I'm always willing to learn from an expert, big brother.'

There were ten questions on the Edinburgh test. For each question there were four options. For questions like *Have you felt worried and anxious for no very good reason?* the options were: *No*; *Not at all*; *Hardly ever*; *Yes, sometimes*; *Yes, very often*. And Sophie had done extremely well. As Miranda had guessed, she had scored top marks on every question. For a slightly older woman who had just given birth, this was more than remarkable.

Jack looked at the results and smiled encouragingly at Sophie. 'You seem to be coping extremely well,' he said.

'No problems at all. Not one.'

'That's good to hear. Husband quite supportive?'

'He's as delighted as I am.'

'And he can manage without sleep just as you can?'

Just for a moment Sophie looked defensive. 'Well, he has to work long hours, you know,' she muttered. 'And we have our own business.'

'Of course. You're just a bit unusual, Sophie. We seldom see women as cheerful as you so soon after the birth of a first child. They're happy, of course—but usually tired as well. I wonder how you keep yourself so bright. Can you give us any reason? We'd really like to know.' Jack smiled encouragingly.

Sophie didn't answer at first. Then she said, 'I'm just lucky, I suppose.'

'Good. Now, I think we'd like to see you again in about a week if that's all right. And one more thing— I'd like the midwife here to take a blood sample.'

'Why do you want a blood sample?' Sophie's voice was suddenly sharp. 'It's been tested enough, there's nothing wrong with my blood.'

Jack's voice was gentle. 'Just a normal precaution. We want to do the best for you and the baby.'

'What will you test for?'

'Anything that might harm you or the baby. Remember, you're still breastfeeding. Anything that you take might pass into the baby's system. Not a good idea. What might we find, Sophie?'

It was a gently spoken question, but it seemed to hang in the air like a threat.

Sophie burst into tears. 'My husband will be so mad! He didn't know. But I was so tired, and so depressed, that I went into the dispensary. I knew what to take and I helped myself. It won't harm the baby, will it?'

'What did you take, Sophie? Don't worry, we can sort things out, but I'd like you to stay here for a night or two and have you talk to some people. And I'm sure your husband won't be too angry with you. Now, what did you take?'

'Amphetamines,' sobbed Sophie. 'Having a baby in the house was harder than ever I thought and I couldn't sleep and I thought just one or two wouldn't hurt. And they made me feel all right.'

'We'll see if we can find something else,' said Jack.

Miranda and Carly had other appointments; it didn't do to keep their patients waiting too long. Jack said he'd see to the admission of Sophie.

'Thanks, Miranda,' Carly said when they had a rare moment of peace together. 'You saw something that I didn't. You were great.'

Miranda shrugged and grinned. 'I'm older than you and I've seen more cases,' she said. 'Another year or so and you'll be able to spot things like that automatically. Anyway, I wasn't sure.'

'I'm learning,' said Carly.

But Jack wasn't so easy to convince. He was waiting for her when she finished her shift. 'Spotting that Sophie was on something was a smart piece of diagnosis,' he said as they strolled down the corridor together. 'She had Carly fooled and she would probably have fooled me if I hadn't been warned.'

'Just experience,' Miranda said uneasily. 'I'm a midwife, I've seen a lot of new mums.'

'You knew she was on something, didn't you? On some drug or other?'

'Yes. Well, I guessed.'

'At some time you must have had quite a bit of experience of that kind of thing.'

She didn't want to carry on with this conversation, it was getting dangerous. She certainly didn't want to carry on with it now, in a hospital corridor. 'You come across all sorts in a hospital,' she said. 'Now, I'm needed in SCBU. See you, Jack.'

CHAPTER FOUR

THAT evening Miranda was alone in the flat when Jack rang her doorbell. She hadn't been expecting him; she was surprised. She was pleased to see him but wished he'd have given her a bit of notice. She was dressed in housekeeping mode—tatty jeans and T-shirt, a scarf around her head. 'Come in, Jack! This is an unexpected pleasure.' She waved at her outfit. 'Sorry about the mess I'm in. I'm fighting the dirt devils.'

He grinned. 'You look fine to me. Nice to see so much of you.'

All right, it was an old and a tight T-shirt. She resisted the urge to fold her arms over her chest and led him to her living room.

He looked at her thoughtfully. 'It's a flying visit. It's just that I got some results a few minutes ago and I thought you might be interested.'

'Results? You could have phoned me.' Then she realised what she had just said and hastily added, 'Though I'm very glad you did come. It's good to see you. What results?'

'Sophie Vesey. We've got the psychiatrist looking at her, she thinks she can sort Sophie out. We checked her blood. If she'd continued taking amphetamines at the rate she was taking them, the results could have been very serious. Especially for the baby. But clever of you to notice how she was.'

There was an invitation there, it was her choice to accept it or not. All right, she was on home ground, she could make a choice. She'd tell him. 'You know I had a car accident. My fiancé was killed by my side. Well, as I recovered…the surgeon in charge of me said that they'd done a fair job of putting my body back together. But…not my brain. The spirit that made me, me…that had been damaged, too. So for a while I was a psychiatric outpatient. And I saw other patients and I got to recognise various kinds of behaviour.'

She didn't know why he did it, but she liked it. He put his arms round her, gave her a quick hug. 'The spirit that made you, you. It's recovered, I can tell.'

'I hope so.' Miranda looked at him in what she thought was a not too challenging way. 'Now, I'm changing the subject,' she said. 'And the mood. I'm glad you called round. I've got a present for you. I've been wondering if I'd ever get the chance to give it to you.'

She went to her bedroom and brought him a small parcel. It was wrapped in gold paper, tied with crimson ribbon and had a large bow on top. He looked at it thoughtfully. 'Why do I deserve a present?'

'Because you took me to the conference. And because I wanted to get you a present.'

He tapped the parcel thoughtfully. 'Why do I suspect that when I open this, I'll get a bit of a shock?'

'Because you are you and I am me. Come on, aren't you curious?'

'I'm curious.' He tore open the packet. Inside was something she had toured the shops to buy. And she was pleased with. He held up what she had bought him. 'A pink shirt!'

'My eyes got tired of looking at all those glistening white shirts that you wear.'

'But I'm not a pink-shirt man! What will people say if they see me in this?'

'They'll say, "There's a man in a pink shirt."' She grinned to herself. 'And he looks cool.'

'Cool! Surgeons don't look cool!'

'Start a trend,' she advised. 'A pink shirt will go very well with the dark suits that you wear. You will wear it, won't you?'

'You bought it for me, so I'll wear it.' He dropped his new present onto the couch. 'Now, I'd better say thank you somehow.'

He put his arms round her and kissed her. Perhaps just a thank-you kiss at first, but it soon turned into something longer and sweeter. Miranda felt odd, both relaxed and excited. With him was like being happy at home, but it was also like wandering into some new and exciting territory. Whatever it was, she had never felt like this with any man before. When he stopped kissing her, she pulled him back closer, kissed him again.

And then there was the noise of the door opening

downstairs. Annie had come home. 'Guess I'd better go,' he said, 'though I'd love to stay.'

By accident she met him in the corridor next day.

'How do I look?' he asked. As ever, when she saw him, her heart beat a little faster. In fact, this time it beat much faster. He looked so different. He was wearing her pink shirt! Still the dark suit, still the college tie, but the shirt really stood out.

'You look great. Really cool. A good start, but there's more progress to be made yet. I think you need to wear a different tie to go with your new look. I'll buy you one.'

'Miranda!' He looked scandalised. 'We have to take this one step at a time. I happen to like my tie.'

'We'll see.' She smiled, her eyes dancing. 'Look, I have to get to work.'

She hadn't expected to see him again so quickly.

But as she carried out the obs and feeding of the four prem babies in her care, she became more and more worried about the condition of Gracie Johnson. Gracie was being ventilated, and at first all seemed to be going well. But then there was evidence of bradycardia and cyanosis. Her heartbeat slowed, her lips were turning blue. The little girl wasn't getting enough oxygen—but why?

Miranda checked the endotracheal tube, which was fine. The air supply was there—if the baby could take it. She went in search of a doctor.

To her surprise, Jack was in the sisters' room, looking through some files. He was wearing a white coat, apparently for a while he was working on the wards. Well, occasionally he did, especially when he was concerned about the welfare of one of the children he had operated on.

Miranda said, 'I'm concerned about Gracie Johnson. I think she has a pneumothorax.'

With some doctors she wouldn't have offered a diagnosis herself. But she knew that Jack would respect her as an experienced professional. Of course, he'd check what she thought. But he'd know that she was almost certainly right. 'Let's have a look,' he said.

They stood together by the incubator. Gracie's condition was worsening by the minute. Jack warmed his stethoscope, listened to the tiny chest and nodded to Miranda. 'Decreased breath sounds on the left side. We haven't time to organise an X-ray. We'll do a needle aspiration first and then get a drain in. You'll assist me?'

'Of course,' said Miranda. 'I have done this before.'

A pneumothorax. For some reason, air was escaping out of one of the infant's lungs and into the pleural cavity. This reduced the lung's capacity—in time might collapse it. And Gracie needed both lungs to survive.

This had to be an aseptic procedure. Miranda fetched gloves and gowns for both of them. Then she cleansed the skin and under Jack's supervision infiltrated a local anaesthetic, lignocaine.

Miranda held the baby still—not that she was capable of much movement now. Jack took a butterfly needle attached to a syringe via a three-way tap. Cautiously, he pushed it into the baby's chest, being ultra-careful not to puncture the lung. There was the faint hiss of air escaping from the pleural cavity. Jack looked up and smiled. The lung would now re-inflate and Gracie could breathe more easily. The emergency was over—but there was more to do.

Miranda assisted as Jack cut through the intercostal muscle, introduced a drain, sutured it into position and then connected it to a Heimlich valve. Now the pneumothorax could heal itself. Any air escaping from the lung would be drawn out at once by the drain.

Jack stood back, looked down at his tiny patient and nodded approvingly. There was a much healthier-looking baby.

'That went well, didn't it?' Miranda asked.

'It did. You knew what I was thinking, could anticipate what I wanted. I enjoyed working with you, we make a good team.'

'In all sorts of ways,' said Miranda, mischievously,

'Very definitely in all sorts of ways. In fact, I was going to suggest—'

'Morning, Miranda. Morning, big brother, sir.'

Miranda turned. There was a smiling Toby. 'Don't let me interrupt any important conversation or a clinical procedure,' he went on breezily, his grey eyes twinkling, 'but I could do with a hand in a minute. I'd like to get an IV line into Baby Halsall.'

'Why does Baby Halsall need an IV line?' Jack asked.

Toby's answer was prompt. 'Not taking enough food. I want to get some glucose into her. Look, here are the weights.'

Jack glanced down and nodded. 'Good. Now, Miranda here has got a bit of clearing up here to do and then she can help you. I need to write up some notes.'

'No hurry. When she's ready. Finish what you're doing, Miranda, and I'll wander around and tell funny stories to the rest of our congregation.'

The joke was, that's exactly what he did. Out of the corner of her eye Miranda could see him peering into the incubators, occasionally reaching in to tickle or stroke a baby or make sure it was comfortable. And whatever he did, he talked to them. She could hear the drone of his voice, occasionally a word or two. She heard him chatting away to a tiny neonate who couldn't have weighed more than a couple of pounds and smiled.

Not all nurses or doctors did this. But Miranda believed firmly that talking to children, no matter how premature they might be, helped them to grow and survive. It seemed that Toby felt the same way.

Eventually she finished writing up her obs on Gracie Johnson and went over to see what he wanted. 'Just hold little Laura while I get this line in. She wriggles and she's slippery. I like my babies to lie there and smile at me.'

'So I've heard,' Miranda said dryly. 'Your bedside manner is renowned.'

He grinned at her. 'I stand reproved. Now, if you hold her…'

They worked well together for a while. Quickly, the IV tube was inserted and the drip installed. Little Laura complained at first but then quickly quietened. And as they stood and watched to make sure that all was working correctly, he said, 'I see that my brother Jack is mellowing, turning into a dandy. Have you seen his new pink shirt? I could fancy one myself. I wonder where he got it from.'

'They've just got them in...' Miranda started, then stopped in confusion.

She realised Toby was laughing at her. But his eyes were shrewd. 'It's one thing to buy my big brother a shirt,' he said. 'It's quite another to make him wear it. What he needs is the love of a good woman. Now you've got him under control, you've got to keep him that way. You will, won't you?'

Miranda jumped as from behind them a stern voice said, 'Toby, I'm sure she will keep me under control.'

She turned and there was Jack, his face as stern as his voice had been. Toby, however, seemed completely unmoved. With a grin he said, 'I'm very glad to hear that, Jack. We all want you to be happy.'

Jack sighed and said to Miranda, 'It's always a mistake to work with relatives. Toby, have you finished here?'

'Now, that's a hint if I ever heard one. Yes, I've finished.' A cheerful Toby walked out of the room.

When Toby had gone Miranda said tentatively, 'He was only joking, you know. About us. About control. I think he's a good doctor.'

'He's always joking. I don't mind it at all. And he'd better be a good doctor, otherwise I'd skin him. But I doubt it will be necessary.'

He pursed his lips, looked down at Laura Halsall and smiled. 'I think we've got things sorted out here,' he said. 'Bleep me if there's another sudden problem, otherwise come and give me a progress report in a couple of hours. I'll have a coffee ready for you.'

'I'd like that,' she said.

He stood there a minute in silence then turned to go. Miranda looked at him, the dark suit, the new pink shirt, the face that she had once thought of as craggy—and a great rush of emotion drove through her. Jack Sinclair was everything she could ever have wished for in a man! But was she all he could ever wish for in a woman?

It was hard, but she forced her attention back to her work. She had a job to do. It would be better to keep her feelings to herself. At least for now.

She sat in Jack's room and drank his coffee. She thought it was typical of the man—the coffee was superb. She'd watched him make it, so carefully. Whatever Jack did, he needed to do well.

'I don't know if you've been listening to hospital gossip,' Jack started, 'not that there's much to gossip about. But I wanted to explain why I've got my brother and sister working in the same department as me.'

'Something about your mother being ill?' Miranda had heard a couple of rumours.

'She has brain-stem cancer and in time she will die.'

Miranda winced at this flat statement, tried to cope with the enormity of what he had told her. 'But it must hurt you! It must affect your work!'

An instant flash of the old Jack. 'Nothing affects my work!' He thought a moment and then went on. 'Toby was in London and Carly was in America when our mother first fell ill. They both gave up their positions and got jobs here. Now they are round at my mother's every spare minute. They've been so good with her. And on the other hand, I think the hospital benefits from them. I don't want anyone to think that they ride on my coat-tails.'

'Just the opposite! If anything, people think that you work them too hard. Jack, how's your mother now?'

He smiled. 'She's in a period of remission. She's gone on a cruise, will be away for at least a month. Her body might be slowing down but her brain is as good as ever.'

'I think it's wonderful, the way the three of you are rallying round.'

'In some ways we're a very close family. But at times Toby's sense of humour can be…'

'I like him! We all like him. On the ward he's always his usual cheerful cheeky self and he wakes us all up.'

'Aren't there times when he should learn not to joke about things?'

'We can all take it. The nurses and midwives prefer him to some of the glum SHOs who seem to think the world is full of misery.' Miranda looked at Jack thoughtfully. 'You know, I can tell you and Toby are brothers. You look a bit alike but, more than that, your characters are similar.'

Jack was astonished. 'We're nothing like each other!'

'Oh, yes, you are. You're both hiding something— the real you. He does it by joking. You do it—used to do it—by pretending to be cold and distant.'

He was silent for a moment. Then he said, 'You're getting to know me too well.'

'It's not too well, it's just getting to know you. If you want me to.'

He didn't answer at first. Instead, he reached across his desk, ran a finger down the side of her cheek. 'I want you to,' he said eventually. 'But much of my life recently I've kept up this attitude. It makes life easier, it makes me a better surgeon. And the way I am, it keeps the neonatal surgical section as one of the best in the country.'

'You've got to be hard and soft at the same time,' Miranda said, grinning. 'And you can do it.'

'Perhaps.'

They sat in silence for a moment, each quite happy just to look at each other. And somehow Miranda knew that he was feeling exactly the same as she was. She felt a great but a simple delight just to be close to him. For a moment no need to speak or to touch. They were together. And there was a communion beyond bodies.

His phone rang and they both jerked to attention. He looked at it gloomily, but both knew it had to be answered.

'Hi, Jenny. Good to hear from you… Yes, I'd like that… Yes, in her own time, and you always have first call… Sure, anyone else who wants to come, you know that's always been the case… Thanks!'

He rang off and smiled broadly at Miranda. 'That was Jenny, your supervisor. As far as possible, she'll let me know when you're working. Then, and only in your own time, you can come and observe me operating. You want to be a scrub nurse, this is the way to learn.'

'Great!' said Miranda.

'This is Charlotte Ramsden, my scrub nurse,' Jack said. 'She's been with me for years and now I don't need to ask her for things, she knows what I need before I do myself. Just sit by her. Watch and you'll learn. You can ask questions afterwards.'

'Right,' said Miranda.

It was in the operating theatre that she had first seen Jack Sinclair and she remembered the wonder she had felt when she had seen what miracles he could work on those tiny bodies. Now she was not just an onlooker. She was part of the process, not an actual worker yet but a trainee.

The first baby was wheeled in. Jack looked around the theatre. 'OK, this is Shauna Whitlock,' he said. 'She has hydrocephalus, and as you will know the fluid produced in the four ventricles of the brain, the cerebro-spinal fluid, is not being reabsorbed. This causes pressure on the brain. So I am going to drill into her skull, introduce a tube with a one-way valve in it so it can tap the CSF. Then we will run another tube just under the skin, down to the peritoneal cavity, where the CSF can be easily absorbed.'

Then, without looking, he stretched out his hand and Charlotte placed a scalpel in it.

Miranda watched, fascinated. She knew Jack now. There was a moment's pause and she noticed the hunched shoulders, the frowning brow. She knew what he was doing, how he was focussing all his attention on the case in front of him. Then he relaxed, made the first cut. Things would be fine now.

Afterwards they sat in the canteen and talked. 'What did you think?' he asked.

It was hard to express what she thought. 'There's something I've always been told,' she said slowly, 'but although I've been told it, I've never felt it. Now I can feel it. I think you're a brilliant surgeon. This is no reflection on you, but you're only as good as your team. You, the anaesthetist, even the scrub nurse…they all are important. You can't manage without them.'

'That's true.'

'So I want more than ever to be a scrub nurse.'

'If you get to be as good as Charlotte, you'll never be short of a job.'

CHAPTER FIVE

SHE didn't see much of him the next week. He'd called her into his office, told her he'd have no time to spare as he was so busy.

She'd walked round his desk, leaned over and kissed him quickly. 'And to show you that you aren't the only busy person in the world—' she grinned '—I'm needed in SCBU right now.'

She did see him every day, but seldom for more than five minutes. It was hard but she was content—and just a tiny bit pleased when she saw he was suffering as much as she was. One day he said something that both excited her and made her slightly apprehensive. 'This time will pass soon,' he said. 'Then we have to move on. We've got things to decide. We have a future.'

A future? She wasn't sure she wanted to think of the future. For the moment she wanted to live for the day. There were things about her that she hadn't told him yet. She was scared.

* * *

Wednesday was a bad day in SCBU. Nurses, midwives, had to be tough, had to take the hard with the joyful. Most of the children they treated managed somehow to survive. Some did not, and on Wednesday two of their precious charges died.

Miranda had to comfort one of the mothers—though what comfort could there be? And although she got some small pleasure from the thought that she might have helped the mother, if even only a little, it was still dreadfully emotionally draining.

She desperately wanted to talk to Jack, just to be with him for a few minutes, just to take strength from him. But she knew it would not be right. He needed all his strength for what he was doing. And she had fought battles like this before.

Then she picked up a call for Jack from Danielle, who phoned to say that things were going well. When Miranda explained that Jack was tied up all week, Danielle recognised Miranda's voice and told her that Wayne was working. She sounded very upbeat and positive, completely different to the first time Miranda had spoken to her.

'Thanks to Mr Sinclair, I really think things are going to be all right,' said Danielle. She hesitated. 'I don't suppose you'd like to come and visit at all, if you're free? Kylie would love to see you again.'

Having had such a difficult day, Miranda decided to spend a happy hour or two with Danielle and the children, and accepted. What to take? A small gift might be pleasant but exactly what? In the end she decided on chocolate. Everyone loved chocolate.

She drove to the estate and parked her car under a lamp. Then she walked to Danielle's flat.

It turned out to be a comfort, being with Danielle. They chatted, and eventually Miranda spoke about the two deaths in SCBU, to get it off her chest. Danielle understood.

'I'm so sorry to hear that. When Mr Sinclair told me what was wrong with Kylie, I just couldn't take it in at first. It wasn't right, it wasn't fair. I'd done everything I could to make sure my new baby was all right. Even gave up smoking when I was having Derek. And that was a strain. Like I said, it just wasn't fair.'

'You were lucky.' Miranda was holding the happily gurgling Kylie on her lap, gently bouncing her up and down. 'And I'm glad for you.'

'I'm glad myself.' Danielle looked at Miranda thoughtfully. 'You like babies, don't you? I can tell. When are you going to have one of your own?'

Miranda tried to keep her face calm. 'Plenty of time yet,' she said. 'I've got to find the right man first.'

'Mr Sinclair isn't married, is he? Could you marry him?'

Miranda laughed, though it sounded a little shrill even to herself. 'He'd have to ask me. But we just work together.'

'Didn't look that way when you called last time,' said Danielle. 'You couldn't keep your eyes off him. Fancy another cup of tea?'

'Love one. Where's Derek tonight?' Miranda wanted to change the conversation.

She left a few minutes later. Danielle had obviously been pleased to see her and Miranda gave her her mobile number. She'd call again. As she walked back to her car she felt much better. It was good to see an obviously content Danielle in her spotless little home. There were some good results. And if Danielle's problems could be solved, why not her own?

Then the week was nearly over. On the Thursday night he phoned her at home. 'Tomorrow night,' he said. 'I'm likely to be working very late, but I expect to be finished at about nine. Would you meet me at the Red Lion? I'll be bushed but I'll be in the mood for a tiny celebration. The hard week will be over.'

'I'll see you there,' she said. 'Look forward to it.'

As the Red Lion was the hospital's local pub, she was quite happy to go there on her own and knew that was why Jack had suggested it. It would be full of people she knew.

She got there quite early, bought herself a glass of red wine and then stood, chatting casually to people she knew. She didn't want to sit down, to join a group. When Jack came, she wanted him on her own.

And then there was a hand on her arm and a voice murmured behind her, 'I've bought you another glass of red wine. And over there are two seats where we can sit together and not be disturbed.'

She turned. It was Jack. He was wearing his usual

smart black trousers and highly polished shoes. But he was also wearing a very sharp designer sweater, in a very un-Jack colour. She couldn't help it. She squeaked, 'Where did you get that sweater from?'

He looked abashed. 'Five minutes ago I told Toby I was coming down here to meet you,' he said. 'And Toby said, "Not dressed like that, you aren't", and made me borrow this sweater.'

'I like Toby. And you look really good in his sweater. Sexy.'

'Thanks. And Toby has his good points.' Jack took her arm and guided her to the vacant table.

She was aware of assorted curious glances, knew that they would be the gossip of the hospital next day. No matter, she didn't mind. And he had taken the decision to meet her here knowingly. He must have known what would happen. Now they were a couple. She was pleased that he had taken the decision.

They sat facing each other, sipping their red wine. 'You look tired,' she said, 'I can tell you've had a hard week.'

Jack shrugged. 'You get a hard week and then an easy one,' he said. 'It's part of my life and I like it. But I've missed seeing you. I feel that something had been started between us but we didn't have chance to carry on with it.'

'I've missed seeing you, too, but I'm a bit frightened of what might happen. Last year my emotions…they took a bit of a battering. It's not easy when the man you think you might marry is killed while sitting next to you.'

He took her hand, stroked her palm. 'I can imagine.

But still, your life must go on.' He grinned. 'And you have re-invented yourself.'

'Sort of re-invented,' she suggested.

'Sort of re-invented, then. Now, I think we've got to know each other quite well, but it's all been a bit casual and work-related. Time for the next step. How would you like to go out with me tomorrow evening? I'd love you to come.'

'Go out with you? You mean, like as on a date?'

'A date?' He winced. 'That would be the last expression I'd use. But I guess that's what I have in mind.'

'Jack, I'd love to go out with you! Where are you taking me?'

He looked smug. 'That is to remain a secret. Shall I pick you up about six?'

He phoned her late the following morning. 'I've just been schooled by my younger man-about-town brother,' he said. 'Not an easy experience. He says I have to tell you not what to wear but the kind of thing to wear. Tonight, he suggests, we are smart casual—whatever that means. He says you'll know.'

'I know,' she said. 'Are you going to be smart casual, too?'

'That depends on whether Toby manages to overcome my long-established prejudices. Is it proper for a consultant to borrow the clothes of an SHO?'

'I think that it's OK if it's in the family,' she said. 'You're not going to give me a hint where we're going?'

'A bit of mystery is good for the soul,' he said. 'Remember, six o'clock.'

Miranda had arranged to go to a trendy hairstylist in town to have her hair streaked and given a simple but sexy style. Then she and Annie set to and looked through both their wardrobes. Smart casual. Something that people would notice and perhaps remember, but also something that appeared to have been put together without much thought. In the end she wore her smart black trouser suit with a rather revealing scarlet silk blouse borrowed from Annie. 'You'll be all right in that.' Annie nodded. 'Just don't bend forward too much. You're a bigger girl than me.'

'Right.'

Now all she had to do was wait for him to call. She'd had her hair done, showered carefully to avoid messing it up and massaged lots of expensive moisturiser into her skin to make it even more silky. She'd dressed and done her make-up. And it was only five o'clock. An hour to wait! Well, she could read.

It was a terrible thing to admit, even to herself, but once again, from half past five onwards she found herself glancing out of the window, waiting for the black sports car to appear at the end of their little cul-de-sac. She felt anxious, excited as a teenager on her first date. Where were they going? What would they do afterwards? Should she invite him back here or would he take her to his flat?

The black car appeared. She flew to the front door—then made herself walk back into the living room. The last thing she wanted was for him to know just how desperately she had been waiting.

The doorbell rang. She walked calmly to answer it. And blinked at the vision that was waiting for her.

'Now, aren't you a lovely sight for a lady's eyes?' she said.

'This is all my brother's work,' he said glumly. 'In fact, it's his suit and shirt. I think he's trying to get his own back for the times I've made him work extra hours.'

'But, Jack, you look wonderful!' She thought for a moment and then added, 'But I must admit—you look different.'

He was wearing a light fawn linen suit, creased to just the right amount, and underneath it a dark blue silk shirt. No tie. And he did look wonderful. She knew that wherever they went that evening, people would be looking at him.

'Something's wrong,' he said. 'I'm dressed for a day by the seaside—and you're in the formal black suit that I usually wear.'

'There are a few differences.'

'There are indeed.' He looked at her scarlet blouse and she resisted the temptation to pull at the collar, ease it upwards. She'd spent half an hour judging precisely the amount of décolletage she should show. 'If I look wonderful, you look magnificent.'

'Shall we go?' she asked. 'I'm feeling excited already.'

They parked in the centre of town; he took her hand and led her through the Saturday evening crowds. The shoppers had gone, now people were out for pleasure.

And she was right. Jack did attract a number of admiring glances.

He took her first to a hotel that specialised in early evening meals for people who were going on afterwards to the theatre, a show or a concert. They had steak and salad—and debated whether it was better to have red wine or champagne with steak. On this night, champagne won. She felt elated, excited. And she was filled with anticipation. In spite of her entreaties, he wouldn't tell her where they were going. She was surprised to learn that Jack could be a bit of a tease.

Then it was time to go. He led her past the market and… 'I still want to know where we're going, what you've—Jack, you haven't got tickets!'

They stood outside the city's largest theatre.

'I have. It took some doing, I had to call in a couple of favours. But we have seats. In fact, we have a box.'

'How did you know that I—?'

'When I was looking through your CDs I noticed that you had more by this fellow than anyone. And he's here for just one night. A quick tour of the provinces, a week in London and then back to America.'

'Jack, you're marvellous! You couldn't have picked anything better for me.' She reached up, kissed him quickly on the cheek. 'Come on, I don't want to miss a second of this.'

Her favourite singer. A man who had been singing for thirty years, and had never yet fallen out of favour. A man who sang about love—as if he had experienced every feeling that it might bring. This was going to be an evening to remember!

It was. Their little box was practically on the stage—she could see him as clearly as if he had been in her living room. She smiled when he sang about the joys of young love, felt the lump in her throat when he sang about love that was unrequited, or undeserved. She let go of Jack's hand just long enough to clap. With the rest of the audience, she stood and cheered. And when the performance finally ended, after three generous encores, she felt overwhelmed with happiness.

'Jack, that was one of the best evenings of my life,' she said. 'Thank you so much for taking me.'

'It was one of the best evenings of my life, too,' he said. 'Because I was with you. Now, after all the emotion, are you hungry again? Or would you like a drink? You told me once that you wanted to try big-city life. This is your chance.'

She couldn't resist the chance of a little dig. 'Are you trying to treat me like one of your women?'

'Certainly not. You're nothing like them. And that's good.'

'That's OK, then.' She thought for a moment. 'Jack, I don't want to go to a club or anything like that. It's not cold—can we go down by the river? I love it at night.'

'Whatever you want. We'll drive down, park by the Albert Dock.'

So they parked, he took her hand and they walked alongside the black flowing river. 'This is peaceful. It's calming,' she said. 'I can see that ship out there, just a row of lights with a dark shadow around them. It's slipping downriver and out of my life. The people on board know nothing of us and our problems. They have their own lives. And it makes any problems we might have seem unimportant.'

'Do we have problems?'

'There's my life so far.' Her voice was reflective. 'I lost the man I was going to marry, nearly died in a car crash and spent months in hospital. In retrospect, all the choices I made were wrong. Who's to say I'm not making wrong choices again?'

'Do you think you are? Making wrong choices, that is?'

'No,' she said after a while, 'but I'm still a bit frightened. I came here intending to start a new life. For a year or two I was going to keep men at a distance. Get more sure of myself. And then I met you.'

'So, on the whole, are you glad or sorry you met me?'

'Oh, glad. No doubt about it—glad, glad, glad. But I can still worry a bit can't I?'

'Just for a while,' he said. 'But not for too long.'

She made up her mind. 'I think I'm getting a bit cold,' she said. 'I'd like to go home now. Would you like to come in for coffee?'

'I'd love to.'

She made him coffee. Annie was out, both of them knew that she was working a night shift. Whatever happened, they would not be disturbed.

While Jack waited in the living room, Miranda went

to her bedroom and changed again, into shirt and jeans. When she returned he had taken off his jacket and there was a CD playing quietly. It was a song she had heard not two hours before. But now it seemed to have an extra resonance. Last time she had heard it, she had seen the singer in person, and she had been holding Jack's hand. It made things different.

She put the coffee-tray on the table, sat by his side on the couch. 'Thank you for a lovely evening,' she said. 'I've enjoyed it so much.'

'So have I. But the evening's not over yet.'

'No, it's not,' she said. 'And I'm so glad.' Would he take that as an invitation? Did she mean it as an invitation? Whatever, there was no hurry. They sat side by side and drank their coffee.

It was so pleasant to be there. The memory of the show and the meal, the lights now low and the music playing. Jack by her side. How could things get better?

He put his arm round her and kissed her. She had been wanting him to, expecting him to, but it was still wonderful when he did. She closed her eyes, felt the strength of his arms around her and surrendered herself to the sheer delight of what they were doing.

At first his lips were firm on hers. Then the tip of his tongue, gently probing, and she parted her lips so he could—she could—more fully enjoy what they were doing.

But it wasn't too comfortable, sitting side by side. And she'd had a long day. So she felt herself sliding down, stretching herself out on the couch, pulling him so he was lying by her side.

It felt so good to be there with him. They were both fully clothed, of course, but she could feel the full length of his body against hers. Through his shirt she felt the swift beating of his heart. His thigh crossed hers and she could feel the hardness of his arousal, and that made her more excited than ever. This was so good! She felt that life was a dream; wonderful things were happening to her without her asking or deserving them.

He leaned back a little, laid her comfortably on her back. Then, one by one, he unfastened the buttons on her shirt. With delicate fingers he pushed the fabric aside, and somehow managed to unfasten her bra at the same time. She was glad she had put on her most dainty underwear.

Now her breasts were naked. His head bent, his lips fastened on one hard peak and then the other—and she gasped with the sheer pleasure of it. There was nothing she had to do now but be herself, be happy. He would make all the decisions. Wherever he wanted to take her, she would gladly go.

So when his hand trailed down the soft roundness of her stomach, under her waistband, below the sheer silk fabric of her knickers, she was happy. He was leading, she would follow.

But then… Perhaps it was a sign of his innate sensitivity. Both of them knew that if he went further there would be no chance of turning back. And so he asked her, 'Miranda…sweetheart, are you sure?'

And for a moment she tried to think instead of feel.

'Jack,' she whispered. Her voice was thick, it was as if

she didn't want to say the words. 'This is so good, you're making me so happy, you're taking me to places where I don't know where I am. But this is more than sex, isn't it?'

His voice was breathless. 'Yes. It's much, much more.'

It was the hardest thing she had ever done. But she pushed his hand aside, somehow managed to sit up. With a weary hand she brushed her hair back. 'I could live with just sex,' she said. 'And I want to. But if this is going to mean any more to you, then we need to stop. Ultimately I would only make you miserable. Jack, you'd better go home.'

He said nothing. For a while he stared at her, and she worried that he hadn't understood, didn't realise that she was doing this for him, not her. Then still without speaking he stood, walked to her bathroom. She heard the running of water.

When he came back his face was still wet. 'Cold water,' he said. 'It's supposed to chill a man's ardour. It didn't work with me. Goodnight, Miranda.'

He left and she was desolate.

He drove home, went straight to the bathroom and showered. Very, very faintly he could smell Miranda on him or on his clothes—a combination of her scent and her own bodily warmth. He wanted to get rid of the smell. It was tormenting him with the sense of what might have been. Miranda was tormenting him. He put on his dressing-gown, poured himself a whisky and sat in his darkened living room to think.

He had never felt this way about a woman before.

The feelings he was having he had tried to dismiss as adolescent—a belief that only she could make him happy, a desperation for her presence, a longing for her that stopped him from sleeping. This wasn't the usual cool Jack Sinclair!

What was he to do about her? No way would she become just one of the women with whom he had had a casual love affair—something that was pleasant but would be soon over without any great regrets. And she was nothing like Veronica—he knew that. For the first time he was genuinely in love. This was a woman he thought he might be able to share his life with. And the thought frightened him. Now, what was keeping them apart? He tried to think about it coolly, dispassionately, the way he had taught himself to think. But he couldn't. An hour before he had glimpsed a happiness that was beyond belief. If he had made love to Miranda—no, if they had made love to each other—then he knew that both of them would have made that final commitment. It might take time but there would be no doubt of the final outcome. They were meant to be together. But she had held back. Holding back had hurt her, he knew this, could feel it. Why? He just couldn't work it out.

He stood, stretched his arms above his head, tautened his body until the muscles ached and the sinews cracked. He was Jack Sinclair, neonatal surgeon, confident and proud of his skills. Problems were there to be solved. He didn't know what the problem was between him and Miranda, but he would find out and they would solve it.

He just couldn't imagine a life without her.

CHAPTER SIX

ON MONDAY morning Miranda was working an early shift. Just before lunchtime Jenny Donovan came in with a message for her.

'I've had a request from Mr Sinclair. He's got a long list. He'll be operating all day. He knows you have the afternoon off so if you're free, he'd like you to observe just one operation, at about three. Scrub up half an hour before.'

'Great!' said Miranda. 'I'm doing nothing that I can't cancel this afternoon.'

Jenny nodded. 'You're a very good midwife and you obviously enjoy the work. Why do you want to be a theatre nurse?'

'It just appeals to me,' Miranda admitted. 'But I don't think I could ever give up midwifery completely.'

Jenny looked at her directly. 'It's personal but I can still ask. Are you interested in being a neonatal theatre nurse or interested in the neonatal surgeon?'

Miranda blushed. 'I've always been interested in

being a theatre nurse. It just wasn't possible where I
came from. And Mr Sinclair has been helpful.'

'Fine,' said Jenny. 'I'll let him know you're coming.'

Miranda felt the first throb of excitement as she started
to scrub up. Jenny's question came back to her and she
thought about it. Was she more interested in being a
theatre nurse or being with Jack?

Probably a bit of both.

She still wasn't sure how they stood. Did he understand why she had asked him to stop on Saturday night?
She hoped so. But he hadn't said much. And he hadn't
called on Sunday.

She saw that he was back to being his cool stern self
when he walked into the theatre. A quick look round, a
nod to everyone there. No special nod for her, and she
couldn't tell from his eyes whether he was smiling or
not. Well, she would see how things were afterwards.
But she desperately hoped that they were all right.

He said, 'Today we have to correct a case of pyloric
stenosis. The exit between the stomach and the duo-
denum was blocked at birth. I shall make sure the
blockage is removed and all should then be well.'

This time she didn't just sit and watch Charlotte.
Instead, she tried to guess what Charlotte would do
next, work out how she pre-guessed Jack's actions. She
got quite a lot right.

When the operation was over and they were leaving
the theatre, he came to speak to her. 'See me in the

corridor on twenty minutes? When we've got changed?' His voice was mild, calm.

'All right,' she said. She tried to be as calm as him but she didn't know if she had succeeded. She wondered what he wanted to see her for.

It was a bit of a surprise when he did meet her—he was still in the black suit, but this time wearing a bright blue shirt. It appeared to be linen and it looked very good on him.

'I like your shirt,' she said.

'Toby bought it for me.'

'Looks good. Why did you want to see me?' She felt happier than any time since he had left on Saturday night. Things between them were going to be all right.

He took her arm, led her down the corridor. 'We've been seen together. People are beginning to gossip.'

'Of course they are. This is a hospital. You'll never stop gossip.'

'Just for once, I don't particularly want to stop it. I want to make a statement, a proclamation. To you and to everyone else. I'd like you to come and have tea with me in the hospital canteen.'

She hadn't expected this. In fact, she hadn't been sure what kind of reception she might get and this invitation rather disturbed her. 'Why?' she asked. 'I'd love to have tea with you, but specially why?'

'On Saturday night I was angry with you. I could see your point. I know you were trying to think of my ultimate happiness. But what you did was make a decision for me. Surely I should have been consulted?'

She hadn't thought of it that way. 'I suppose so,' she said cautiously.

'And I thought we had an agreement. We were going to see how things progressed. Take things easy, get to know each other.'

'You were doing a bit more than getting to know me on Saturday night,' she pointed out with a grin.

'I was indeed. And I was thoroughly enjoying it. But let's get back to the main point. I want to know you better. To hell with the future, I want today.'

She sighed. 'When you'd gone on Saturday night, I was so miserable,' she said. 'But I was vaguely proud of myself. I'd done something right and proper. I'd thought of you rather than me. And now I'm going to have tea with you and it'll spoil all my good intentions.'

'A shared meal in the hospital canteen is not a major commitment.'

'It will be to everyone watching,' she said. 'Still. Let's get a tray and join the queue.'

There was no doubt, they were being noticed. She noticed curious eyes, half-hidden smiles. And they found a table to themselves. 'Will anyone join us?' she asked.

'I hope not. The last thing I want is a conversation about medical affairs.'

No one did join them. Which was, for her, an unusual occurrence. Even Annie passed them with a quick smile and went to sit on her own. 'I think we've started something,' Miranda said.

'Good. Well, I think it's good.' He picked up his fork

and began to push salad about his plate. 'You know I've had affairs before, Miranda.'

'Well, surprise me,' she said sardonically.

'Quite so. But now things seem to be different with you. There seem to be different ground rules. And of all things, my family is mysteriously taking an interest in you. That has never happened before. Both Toby and Carly have been asking about you. So far, I've kept my social life away from them. But now they want to know all about you and me. And it's hard to deal with.'

She felt a thrill, half excitement, half pride. 'Do you like this interest?'

He had to think. 'I wasn't looking forward to it, but now, yes, I suppose I do. And it's all because you tried to blackmail me. Make me a nice man when I didn't want to be one.'

'You always were a nice man. You just didn't want to show it.'

'Perhaps.' He looked at her as yet untouched lunch. 'Why aren't you eating your salad?'

She picked up her fork. 'Because I'm more interested in talking to you.'

For a while they both ate. Then she said, 'You know, I envy you your family? All mine are over in New Zealand and…well, we've just drifted apart. It must be wonderful having people so close who are really interested in you.'

'And so feel they are entitled to interfere?' he asked with a grin.

'Better to be interfered with than ignored. They do

it because they love you. And you love them back, don't you?'

'I just try not to let them see it too much,' he said. 'But, yes, I love them back.'

It seemed that Miranda was fated to have conversations with the Sinclair family in the canteen. The next day she walked in for an afternoon cup of tea and was waved to by Carly, who was sitting alone.

'I could do with a bit of company,' said Carly. 'Things on the ward have been a bit fraught. We've got a screaming mother and a weeping father and there's just nothing you can do for them. Sometimes it's almost more than I can bear. Being a doctor, distancing yourself from emotions—it doesn't always work.'

'It seems to work for Jack.' Miranda smiled.

Carly smiled back. 'I like a girl with a sense of humour. But I suspect Jack feels as much or more than we do. He just hides it well.'

'Very well.'

Carly leaned over the table, tapped Miranda's wrist. 'He's my big brother. In effect, he's a father figure, too. He's nine years older than us, and he takes being a brother very seriously. We, Toby and I, said we wanted to be doctors at fifteen or so...you should have seen the way he made us work. And we love him for it. Don't mess about with Jack or you'll have the entire Sinclair clan to fight.'

'Me mess with Jack? Sometimes he terrifies me! And he has the whole department just where he wants it.'

'That's because he wants to get things right,' Carly said. Then she added quietly, 'You're not going to mess him about, are you?'

'I don't want to. I think… I think… I think I'm…'

'It's hard to say, isn't it?' Carly asked gently. 'And he doesn't make it any easier. Anyway, let's change the subject.'

'Tell me about your work in Chicago,' Miranda suggested.

Carly's eyes sparkled. 'It's fantastic stuff! Microsurgery like you've never seen it done before. It's going to revolutionise medicine. We can work on blood vessels, nerves—anything. Remember reading about the first heart transplants? Well, it's going to be bigger than that. Some of the techniques are a bit risky but…here.'

She rummaged in her handbag, brought out an American medical magazine. 'You can borrow this for a week. It'll show you the kind of things that they're trying to do.'

'You're going back there?' Miranda asked.

Carly's face clouded. 'In time,' she said. 'When the situation with my mother has…sorted itself out.'

Later, Miranda was in the obs and gynae department, and looked up to see a man wandering around. She didn't know who he was but he seemed to be very important. You could tell by the suit, the tie, the way he held himself. What was he doing?

'Could I help you, sir?' she asked politely.

'I'd be pleased if you could, Midwife…Gale?' The

man had peered at the pass hanging round her neck. 'My name is George Allen.' There was a pregnant pause. The man obviously expected to be recognised. When Miranda didn't respond he added, slightly irritated, 'I'm the hospital CEO. I'm looking for Mr Sinclair.'

'He's in the doctors' room. I'll show you the way there.'

Miranda strode down the corridor. She knocked and opened the door for the important Mr George Allen. Without thanking her, Mr Allen strode through. And just as Miranda closed the door, she heard him say, 'Jack, you've got to change your mind.'

Miranda knew it wasn't her business. What she was about to do was highly improper and she suspected that she could be sacked on the spot for it. But she suspected Jack might be…well, not in trouble, but likely to get in trouble. The hospital CEO had said exactly the wrong thing. If he and Jack were going to argue, Miranda wanted to know why. If there was a problem, she wanted to help Jack.

The linen store was right next door to the doctors' room. She knew just below the ceiling there was a ventilation brick between the two rooms. She had half heard conversations when in there before. So she went to the linen room, moved aside a bag of sheets, climbed up a couple of shelves and pressed her ear to the brick.

Unashamedly, she was going to eavesdrop. She wondered if the CEO was capable of outmanoeuvring Jack—or if Jack could be bothered to try to outmanoeuvre the CEO. Whatever, she wanted to help.

'This truncus arteriosus repair you've agreed to,

Jack,' the CEO was saying. 'I think you should give up the idea. First, it's not your case, it should be handled by a Welsh trust. Second, you're not a neonatal cardiovascular surgeon. You're out of your area of expertise. Third, if the baby dies, it's bad for the hospital's reputation and bad for yours, too. The hospital might lose the chance of getting any extra funding.'

'So I just walk away from it?' Jack asked mildly. 'Look, this is an urgent case. That baby's going to die anyway unless someone does something. And for various reasons there just isn't a neonatal cardiovascular surgeon available at the moment. I've studied all the preliminary material. I've seen X-rays, had an echocardiographic examination, seen an angiography and the results of a cardiac catheterisation. I think I can do the job.'

'It's your decision, Jack. But I'm afraid I'm going to have to put it on record—it's a decision I don't agree with. I've got to cover myself.'

'Your choice, George. That child is in danger of pulmonary over-circulation and heart failure. I'm going to put that right. My reputation, the hospital's reputation—they'll both have to take their chances.'

There was the sound of a door slamming and Miranda turned. It wouldn't do to be found halfway up the wall of the linen store. Unfortunately, she turned too fast. Her heel caught in the wooden slats and with a little squeak of dismay she fell backwards, pulling bags of bedding with her. Even more unfortunately, there were some old tin bowls at the end of one of the shelves. The rattle they made as they fell could have been heard yards away. And certainly in the doctors' room.

Before she could collect herself, the door to the linen store was wrenched open. Fortunately—or unfortunately—it was Jack. He sounded concerned. 'Miranda, are you all right? I heard the crash. I wondered what had happened.'

Miranda pulled down her skirt, tried to look dignified and not guilty. 'I'm fine, thank you. I was…I was looking for some sheets and I fell.'

He glanced round the little room, considered the piles of linen of the floor then looked at her thoughtfully. 'You were looking on the top shelf? Well, as you wish. Come on, I'll give you a hand up and then we can put everything back together.'

She might have got away with it. But there was the sound of a door slamming and from next door, wonderfully clearly, they both heard the sound of a male SHO's voice. 'I need coffee but I haven't time to wait for it to take effect. Do you think you could give me some intravenously?'

A female voice said, 'Would it mix with the alcohol already in your bloodstream?'

Jack looked round the room, fixed on the ventilation brick. Then he looked at Miranda.

All right, she'd own up. But not in the linen store. People could overhear what was being said. With a finger she beckoned Jack to come into the corridor. Once there… 'I was eavesdropping,' she whispered. 'I wanted to hear what the CEO had to say to you.'

His voice was cool. 'You know I can't approve of that, Miranda.'

'The man had that look in his eye, as if he was about to play some cunning trick. All he wants to do is make sure he's not to blame for anything. I'm on your side, I wanted to hear what he said so perhaps I could help.'

'You don't think I can fight my own battles?'

'You can fight battles. What you can't do is hospital management infighting. You just can't be bothered. Can you?'

He shook his head. 'Miranda, with you on my side, I don't need to be an expert infighter. Now, you know I can't at all approve of junior staff trying to overhear the conversations of senior members of staff.'

'Sorry,' said Miranda, trying to look contrite and not succeeding very well. 'I'm afraid this is the new me. I don't back away from fights. In fact, I look for them.'

'You're telling me. However, it strikes me that this should be a disciplinary offence. I could blackmail you.'

'Into being pleasant?'

'Much more than pleasant,' he said, and she blushed.

'Tell me about this truncus arteriosus repair. Why are you particularly interested?'

He looked a little shamefaced. 'It's one of the most foolish reasons I've ever heard for offering to do an operation. Incidentally, the CEO is right. It isn't my responsibility.'

'But you're going to because…?'

'Little Gareth is a twin. He has a sister, Megan, who is perfectly OK. And I feel that there's something special about them, something special about their relationship. I want to preserve that if I can. Carly and Toby are twins and they're very different. But they've got a closeness that I can only envy. They're always there for each other.'

She was curious. 'Do you feel shut out?'

'Not shut out and we're all good to each other. But I know I'll never have that special closeness that they have and at times it upsets me.'

He was silent a moment and then he said, 'I'm going to mid-Wales for a day to study Gareth and talk to his doctors. Then if we agree that the operation is viable, and now is the time to do it, I'll perform the operation here. It'll be a big performance—there'll be all sorts of people in the theatre. And I want you to be one of them.'

'I can't be in the theatre! I can't do anything!'

'You can be there for me,' he said. 'Will you be?'

'All right,' she said.

That night she read up about truncus arteriosus repair. It was a congenital heart anomaly and if it wasn't put right—preferably as quickly as possible—then the child would almost certainly die within a year. There was a hole between two chambers in the heart, too little blood was travelling round the body. Jack would have to open the heart, commit a common arterial trunk to the left ventricle and reconstruct the right ventricle. Not an easy job on such a tiny body.

An operating theatre was no place for nerves and usually Jack had none. But this time he had to admit to a certain trepidation. The operation was complex and it was risky. No one quite knew what might happen, what pitfalls there might be.

He would be under observation. There would experts in the theatre with him, ready to offer advice or even take over if necessary. There would be a crowded gallery watching him. And the whole operation would be recorded. If he made a mistake, he could watch it on playback. Again and again and again. But he didn't mind the CCTV camera. The film might be a good teaching tool. And someone might learn from his mistakes.

Stop thinking about mistakes! He was going to do this right!

His preparation had been rigorous, and there was nothing that could be learned that he didn't now know about Gareth's condition. He took one last breath and strode into the operating theatre.

The twins were already there; he looked round at his team. Calm eyes looked back at him. Then he looked round at the rest of the room, the onlookers. And there was Miranda—like him, masked and gowned. He could see her eyes and knew she was smiling at him. Their glances met and he felt strengthened.

He looked down. Focus! And in a moment Miranda was forgotten. Everything was forgotten. The only thing that existed was the tangled mass of blood vessels, nerves and tissue below him.

He stretched out his hand and Charlotte put the right scalpel into it.

* * *

He was nearly there. The last, most difficult cut and
stitching and then he could start to close. Everyone
round the table knew it. He could feel the tension,
although no one said a word. For the first time in a
couple of hours he lifted his gaze from the tiny baby
below him and glanced around the theatre. There was
Miranda. For a moment it was like the communion
between his brother and sister. She knew what he was
thinking, feeling. And the return message was perfectly
clear. *I have confidence in you, you can do it. Just have
confidence in yourself.*

He made the cut, started the stitching. All was well.
There was a half-heard sigh of relief from those around
the table. But he didn't pay any attention. Things were
now going his way. He was going to succeed!

He did.

He had never heard it before. As he walked out of the
theatre he was clapped. Just like a matinee idol! He
examined his own feelings and was rather surprised. He
was proud of himself.

There were people to talk to, congratulations to be
accepted. It was interesting that the CEO was outside
and was one of the first to congratulate him. 'Our reputation will have gone up tremendously,' he said, 'and
it'll be due to you.'

Our reputation? Jack thought. But he was too tired,
too relieved to argue.

There were invitations to be refused. No, if he could
be excused, he was tired. All he wanted now was his
bed. Tomorrow there would be time for explanations,

evaluations, a running through of what had been done and what could be learned from it.

He had already made sure that overnight Gareth would get the best of nursing care. He had absolute confidence in the SCBU staff. For now he could hand over responsibility.

He showered, changed, walked into the corridor and, as he knew there would be, there was Miranda waiting for him. 'What you did was beautiful,' she said. 'So beautiful that I nearly cried.'

'Beautiful?'

'That was the word I used and I meant it. Now you look weary.'

'I am,' he said. 'But I want to see you and—'

'I have a suggestion. I've never been to your flat and I'd like to see it. You go back there. I'll come round later and bring a Chinese meal for us both. Annie has told me of a place that's fantastic. How's that for an idea?'

'I can't think of anything better,' he said. And he felt a throb of anticipation.

Jack had given Miranda a card with his address and later that evening she drove round to his flat. There was a leather bag over one shoulder and she carried a take-away Chinese banquet in a large cardboard box.

The address led her to a large Edwardian house in extensive gardens, she saw that it had been converted into three flats. Vaguely she had imagined that he would live in some kind of bachelor flat—nothing as palatial as this.

When she rang his bell he came down to open the

door in person. He was wearing a blue short-sleeved shirt, light-coloured trousers and had bare feet. 'So you can relax!' she exclaimed. 'I've hardly ever seen you out of a suit before.'

'A man has to take things easy sometimes,' he said reproachfully. 'Come on in and look around.'

She was amazed by the flat. The living room was large, elegantly proportioned. There was a mahogany-surround fireplace, with a coal-effect gas fire. There was a polished oak floor covered with a rich red rug and matching red velvet curtains. Not too much furniture but everything there was in keeping.

'This is a beautiful home,' she said.

'I like surrounding myself with beautiful things.'

There were watercolours on the walls, Lalique glass on the mantelpiece. A great leather couch faced the fireplace. It was a room that fitted his personality perfectly. The first impression was of good taste, of order. Then there was the feeling of passion underneath.

'I see you've brought dinner,' he said, pointing to her carrier bag. 'Shall I fetch plates?'

'No. First, we don't want the smell of cooking in this lovely room and this is only a take-away. Can we eat in the kitchen off ordinary plates?'

'This way,' he said.

She might have guessed that the kitchen would be super-modern. Grey slate floor, island cooker, a wall of high-tech stainless-steel units. Miranda thought of the pleasant but cramped little room where she shared meals with Annie, and grinned. But this place didn't look very used. 'You don't do much cooking?' she asked.

He grinned back. 'I don't have time. But what I can do, I do very well.'

'And that is?'

'Sandwiches and coffee. And I can pull the cork out of a bottle of wine.' He pulled open a stainless-steel drawer. 'And I have warmed some plates.'

They ate. She had little idea of what she was eating, just a vague impression that it was rather good. He fetched them a bottle of iced beer each; that, too, she felt was rather good. But mostly she was happy just to be there and to be with him.

'Do you want to talk about the operation?' she asked.

He shook his head. 'It's over now. If there's any problem tonight, I'll be contacted. But all should be well. Tomorrow there'll be people to meet, discussions on technique and so on. And I'll want to evaluate what I did. But for now I want just to be with you.'

It was then that she realised just what the afternoon had taken out of him. To her he had always been the macho male—quick to make difficult decisions, unworried by problems, confident in his own abilities. Now, just for once, she saw him as a man who could tire, who could even doubt himself. It made him more human. More lovable.

So they didn't talk too much as they ate. But she was happy to be with him, to smile at him, to let her hand trail over his as she handed him yet another foil box. He needed to relax.

When the meal ended she stacked dishes in the washer and threw away the debris while he percolated coffee and poured two large glasses of brandy. Then they went into his living room.

They were sitting side by side on his couch. They had finished the coffee and were sipping the brandy. She had kicked off her shoes, was half sitting, half lying against him. She was happily comfortable. She had made a decision. What its consequences might be she just wouldn't think about. But then the power of making decisions was taken from her. He leaned towards her, took her two hands in his.

'Miranda?'

Just her name, one word, but it made her sit up at once. Whatever it was, what he was about to say was important. He was looking at her, eyes intent. Then he nodded thoughtfully, almost as if he'd made some sudden discovery. 'You'll have to tell me now,' he said. 'We have to move on.'

'Tell you what?'

'I'll put it a gentler way. I'd like you to tell me now.'

Her voice was quavering, she didn't know how to stop it. 'I still don't know what you're talking about.'

She tried to ease her hands away from his, but he wouldn't release her. Instead, he turned to face her, his expression intent. 'I know you're hiding something from me. And I suspect that it's not as bad as you think. I'd like you to tell me what it is.'

She wrenched her hands from his. 'There's nothing!

And, anyway, I'm the one who gets people to talk about their problems. You're the one who operates and who keeps people at a distance!'

He nodded. 'Possibly. And you're the outgoing type. You're full of fun, you're popular. You're known to be good at your job. You've only been in the hospital a short time but you're everyone's friend. But I've watched you. There's something in you that I've recognised, and other people have not. There's a sadness in you.'

She was staring at him, open-mouthed. He went on, 'It's your story. You only have to tell me if you want to. But I want you to.'

Miranda thought that this was a completely new Jack Sinclair. It was frightening. He was far more subtle than she had ever realised. She had thought she had kept her secret from him—but he had suspected something all along. Of all her new friends, only he had worked out that there was something wrong.

She sat by his side, her hands clasped in her lap, her head bowed. Then she stood, went to the hall where she had left her leather bag and came back clutching a red plastic folder. She placed it on his lap. Then she mumbled, 'I've been carrying that around for too long. I've been meaning to show it to you but it's…it's never been the right time and I've never dared and…you can look through it in a minute.'

She tried to keep the agony out of her voice. 'Jack, you did say you wanted four children?'

Not his fault, but he completely missed the point of

question. He smiled broadly. 'I certainly do want four children. But I'd settle for three or five.'

The wrong answer. 'We'll talk about children in a minute. But, first, you're a doctor, aren't you?'

'I certainly am.'

'You've seen naked women before—seen them as cases rather than women?'

'I hope so. That's what doctors try to do.'

'Right, then. One picture is worth a thousand words. And a demonstration is worth a thousand pictures.'

Crossing her arms, she pulled her shirt over her head. Then she unbuckled the belt of her jeans, wriggled them to the floor and stepped out of them.

His voice was alarmed. 'Miranda, what are you doing?'

'All right, Jack. This is just a demonstration.' She walked to stand in front of him. For a moment she was vaguely glad that she still was wearing newly bought and pretty underwear. Matching bra and knickers trimmed with a delicate pink lace. Then she decided it didn't matter. This wasn't to be any kind of sexual encounter.

'I'm not getting undressed to excite or invite you. I'm doing it for something very different and I want you to pay attention. Look at this scar.'

She had seen the flare of passion in his eyes when first he had seen her in her underwear, but now that expression disappeared. 'I see the scar,' he said. His voice was neutral now.

He looked at her, saw a V-shaped scar that plunged across her lower abdomen to disappear into the top of her brief knickers. Absently, he went on, 'There is evidence of suturing. The scar is jagged, it's obviously trauma from an accident. But there is also some evidence of surgical intervention.'

He lifted his hand, dropped it again.

'You can palpate if you want.'

'I didn't want to palpate, I wanted to touch. There is a difference. You told me you were in a car crash, Miranda. It was obviously a bad one.'

'Yes, I was in a car crash. I got spiked on one of the windscreen pillars. And I was the lucky one. I lost a lot of blood and I had to have surgery. In fact, I was lucky to survive.'

Now this was the hard part and she felt the tears welling into her eyes. 'Look where the gash was, think what's underneath! What is delicately called my reproductive system. And it had a great steel bar pushed right through the middle of it. Lots of blood vessels, nerves, various other tubes got cut, smashed. The surgeon stitched me together as best he could, but he couldn't repair everything. The uterus is fine. In fact, I still have periods—isn't that a joke! But there was so much damage that I can never have children. And I love them! Sometime I ache for them!'

And now for the final, obvious declaration. 'Jack, I could never have your children!'

He stood, pulled her to him and held her in a grip that half promised that everything would be well. His lips found her cheek; he kissed the tears now streaming down her face. It was a while before he spoke, and when he did the tenderness in his voice made her cry again.

'My poor Miranda. God, how I feel for you. Here, sit by me. You don't have to talk, just let me hold you.'

She did as he said. He put his arms around her and she curled up to him, longing for the feel of his body but wanting comfort rather than passion. And he was comforting. 'I'll just lie here,' she murmured, 'but you're to look through that folder.'

'What is it?'

'A copy of my case notes. Please, I want you to just glance through it. I want you to know everything.

So she lay there and dutifully he scanned the contents of the red folder. Then he tossed it onto the floor. 'Miranda, Miranda,' he whispered. 'This is just the account of a terrible accident. But now you are well. You've recovered.'

'Some of me is recovered. Some of me is still damaged. And that wound will never heal. You can wound the spirit as well as the body, Jack.'

'You're strong enough to recover from any wound. Wound to the spirit or the body.'

It was so good to lie with him but she knew she had to move on. She wriggled out of his arms, reached for the brandy decanter and poured some into their now empty glasses. She handed a glass to Jack, raised the other to her own lips. 'You've had a shock,' she said. 'Perhaps it wasn't fair of me to tell you just after you'd finished that operation. It's been hard on me, talking to you. And I'm going to make it harder. Jack, not ten minutes ago you told me that you wanted four children.

You'd settle for three or five. Now you know. I can't give you any. Jack, we have no future.'

'Oh, yes, we have! Miranda, I can't imagine a future without you. I need you and you need me! Children or not, we are going to be together!'

This was the old Jack back. In a way it was comforting to hear that absolute certainty, to know that obstacles were there merely to be overcome. But this occasion was different.

She stopped, gave him a deep, soul-searching kiss. 'You can do something for me,' she said. 'We forget everything till tomorrow. No arguments, no plans, no promises. We just have tonight and each other. I want to stay with you. Jack, I so much want to stay with you. Where's your bedroom?'

'Across the hall. There's an *en suite*. Shall I—?'

'You give me fifteen minutes. Then come to bed.'

She had told him. It had been as simple, as easy—and as painful—as that. But she had the feeling that some kind of great decision had been made, that after tonight things between them would never be the same. What kind of future could they…? She decided not to think of the future. For now she would live for the day—or the night.

But, still, she was frightened. Just a little.

His bedroom was just as she might have expected it to be. A double bed—fortunately. A comfortable room, elegant but lived in. There was subdued lighting, a glorious golden rug on the floor, a pile of books by the bed. A set of photographs of his mother and the twins. She felt at home here.

In her leather bag she had brought all that she might need. Her toiletries, a change of underwear, even a blue lace nightie she had bought but never worn. A frivolous purchase. Was she going
to need a nightie? She blushed at the thought.

A quick shower in his bathroom—another high-tech room—the usual night-time routine. She contemplated her nightie, then left it tumbling out of her bag. There if she needed it. One bedside lamp left on. Then she slipped into his bed.

He came on time. Her voice shook a little as she said, 'Sometimes I think we spend too much time talking. So don't say anything, just get ready and come to bed with me.'

'Miranda, I—'

'Jack, I'm waiting here for you.'

He came out of the bathroom in a short towelling gown. 'You'll be too hot in that. Take it off,' she mumbled. Then she looked at the ceiling as the bed swayed and his naked body slid in beside hers.

He kissed her—a demanding, passionate kiss that told her of his desperation, his hunger for her. His body pressed against hers. She felt the hard muscles of his arms, chest and thighs, felt his obvious need for her. She could smell the freshness of his body, hear his deep breathing. And her own body responded. She felt the tightness in her breasts, the soft warm moistness between her legs.

'Jack,' she muttered, her voice hoarse, 'I can feel the tension in you. I know what you want. I know you're a kind, sharing man. But now, now I just want to give myself to you. Jack, I want you quickly.'

His voice was hoarse, too. 'Sweetheart, I want to share—'

'Please, Jack. Now!'

He needed no further encouragement. She felt swept away by his sheer masculinity, managed to anticipate his every need, moved her body in time with his so she could give him just what he needed. And so quickly came that echoing cry as he reached a frenzied climax.

She smiled in the semi-darkness.

Now he lay half-across her, his chest heaving, his body heated. She curled her fingers in his hair, kissed him gently on the cheek. With her spare hand she stroked his back.

'You're wonderful to me,' he said.

'And you're wonderful to me, too. Now, go to sleep.'

A moment later he had done just that. And she smiled again.

CHAPTER SEVEN

SHE slept well. Next morning Miranda thought she woke early but to her vague dismay, when she reached out to Jack, he had disappeared. She flicked on the bedside light, sat up to look around. No Jack.

The bedroom door opened. He walked in, dressed in the towelling gown, carrying a tray. And the most wonderful smell was coming from the tray. Coffee!

Modestly, she pulled up the bedclothes to cover herself. He put the tray on the bedside table, leaned forward and pulled the bedclothes down again. 'I can't think of anything I'd rather see first thing in the morning,' he said, then quickly kissed her. 'We'll have coffee in bed.'

'I should have brought you coffee in bed. Then we could have pretended it was your birthday.'

'It nearly is my birthday. Just four days to go.'

'Good. I'll buy you a card.'

His voice was flat. 'Don't bother. It's not something I care to celebrate.'

An odd reaction, she thought. But some men were like that.

A second later, he was the old Jack. He climbed into bed with her, kissed her again and then passed her a coffee. It tasted as good as it smelt.

'Last night was the most wonderful thing that ever happened to me,' he said. 'But now we really ought to talk.'

She kissed him. 'Doing things is more important than talking about them. We're still finding our way, we're going to have to trust each other that things will turn out right. We're going to tell each other things, now you know what my big secret was.'

He nodded. 'All right. But you've given me something so precious that I want to make sure that I keep it for ever. Miranda, you know you could have told me before? Things would have been the same between us.'

'I was frightened of losing you,' she confessed. 'I would have told you eventually, but each time I tried...well, I thought I'd allow myself one last day. Now...' Her cup clinked as she set it on the bedside table. 'It's early. What time do we really have to get out of bed?' she asked seductively.

He put down his own cup, reached for her. 'Not for a while yet.'

She was still a midwife on the bank, and today she had been sent to the delivery suite. This was work she liked. There was something deeply satisfying about helping a mother have her baby. All right, it was a sweaty, difficult, even painful process. Mothers took to it differently. Some apparently thought the midwife was responsible for their pain. But Miranda could ride that out. The look on a mother's face when she first had her baby laid on her breast. Miranda never tired of the sight.

In time the birth was over, the mother moved into the postnatal ward, smiling at the tiny scrap of humanity in the cot by her side. And Miranda could have a much-deserved drink. She went to the nurses' room and poured herself a coffee.

Now she had time to think of her night with Jack. It had been so good. In some strange spiritual way they fitted together—what pleased him pleased her. Nothing made her happier than making him happy. And she knew he felt the same way.

She thought of his birthday. He had said that he didn't celebrate it himself. Well, she would do it for him and they would enjoy it together. The question was how. And as she wondered, Toby came into the room.

He greeted her as he greeted so many people, a big beaming smile, an arm round her waist to give her a quick squeeze. He was pleased to see her, that was all. And now she was pleased to see him.

'Toby, a quick question. Which are the three best men's outfitters in town? And do they stay open late?'

Toby looked awe-struck. ' Not Jack? You're going shopping for him?'

'No. I'm going to take him shopping.'

Toby shook his head in disbelief. 'To think I should see this day.' He took out his notebook, wrote down three addresses. 'These are the best places I know.'

She looked critically at the list. 'They'll do very well,' she said. 'I hope he doesn't take too much persuading.'

'Just tell him that the sweater he so much admired came from the first shop. And he'll be hooked. What he really needs is—'

The door opened and in came Annie. She smiled at Miranda then her eyes flicked to Toby. 'Hi, you two,' she said casually. 'I wanted a coffee but now I remember where my notes were and I'll have to fetch them. See you.'

'Eat more fish,' Toby advised her. 'It's very good for the memory.'

'I'll remember that.' And Annie was gone.

Miranda looked thoughtfully at Toby—who was staring at the door and had suddenly lost his smile.

'Weren't you…close to Annie once?' she asked.

'Not close… Near might be a better word,' he said. 'Just for a while. I think Annie's a wonderful girl.'

Miranda wondered if she detected a touch of desolation in his words.

Jack was operating for most of the day. When she heard that he was back she went to his room. 'I've been wandering around with a silly smile all day,' she said. 'I still don't believe it. Did last night really happen? Will you kiss me again to prove that it did?'

He wrapped his arms round her, kissed her. Not a desperate, passion-led kiss—after all this was in the hospital—but the gentler kiss of one certain lover to another.

'It happened. And I feel a bit apprehensive. Things are going too well for me.'

'Don't worry, things can get even better.' She kissed him back. 'I'm going to take you out to celebrate on

Saturday, when it's your birthday. Don't worry. It's not a birthday present, it's a *you* present. And it'll be a surprise.'

He still didn't seem too happy, but she ignored that. He'd come round.

'What about this evening?' he asked. 'Doing anything? If you want, we could—'

'I've got plans for you. The shops are open late tonight, we're going shopping for clothes. I'm turning you into a new man.'

'But I've already bought six coloured shirts!'

'We're taking things a step further.'

Saturday. Jack's birthday. She was taking him out, but this was not to be a birthday present. She still had a card in her handbag and if she thought the time appropriate, she would give it to him. But for the moment, this was just a day out.

He had said he didn't care to celebrate his birthday. She thought she knew why—birthdays meant other people making a fuss of you. And he liked to keep his distance from most people. Well, he did at the moment. But things were changing.

She had arranged to pick him up at his flat in the early afternoon. It was her treat so they'd go in her car. They were lucky with the weather. Although it was autumn, it was a glorious mild day. Just the kind of day for what she had in mind.

She had a surprise for him. They were going on a cruise up the River Weaver. She'd heard about it from another midwife who had said it was wonderful.

He came out of his flat in his new casual clothes, which they had bought together. Cord trousers, thin sweater, a leather jacket. He looked good enough to eat.

A quick kiss to say hello and they were on their way. 'Where are we going?' he asked.

'Told you. It's a surprise. Surprises are good for you.'

'Whatever you say. I'm in your hands.'

'We seem to have a lot in common. I think what I like you'll like.'

'You've already proved that. When you stayed the night.' She had to blush.

She felt warm and wonderful when she caught him looking at her in that appreciative way. And when they stopped at traffic lights, he stroked her hand. A small caress, but so welcome.

'When I first qualified as a midwife,' she told him, 'a gang of us went out together and we had a fantastic time. Well, I'm trying to recreate that feeling. Just a bit. Only it'll be more fun just the two of us instead of a couple of dozen.'

They drove out of town, over the great arched Runcorn bridge and down towards the motorway. Then she turned off across the greenness of the Cheshire plain. Eventually they came to a small town, and she navigated her way through it cautiously. 'I'm looking for a sign that shows the way to the marina,' she told him.

So far they had chatted happily but now he became quiet. 'Where are we going?' he asked. 'I need to know.'

Need to know? Seemed an odd thing to say, she thought. And his voice was different.

'A special not-birthday treat for you,' she said. 'A boat trip up the river.'

A very long pause. 'That's great. An interesting idea.'

She could tell that he was trying to hide his feelings but he wasn't succeeding. He wasn't happy. By now she was wondering. 'Jack, are you all right about going on the water? You won't get seasick you know.'

'Of course not, And of course I'm all right about the water. No problem.'

Her unease increased. She drove into the marina forecourt. There were rows of barges, an office, a small café. It all looked rather pleasant. But when he got out of the car Jack looked even less enthusiastic than he had sounded. In fact, there was a touch of whiteness on his cheeks.

'The scenery will be wonderful,' she said, aware that her voice was now slightly shrill. 'It's a nice time to come. There's a bar on board, we can have a drink as we travel. And there's a meal served when we're halfway there.'

'Sounds good.'

She wasn't having this. Something was wrong and she was determined to know what. They had decided. No secrets between them.

She took his hand, pulled him away from the car, round the back of the café where there was a bench they could sit on. It was secluded, no one could hear or see them. She took his hands, made him look at her. For once his expression was defensive.

'Jack, you mean a lot to me. I thought that we were getting together, that the old, distant Jack had gone. But

I want to know and you're shutting me out. Jack, you owe me this. What's wrong?'

'It's a bit hard to talk about,' he said. 'I try to forget about it, but I'm not doing a good job today.'

It was the first time she had ever heard him sound uncertain. 'It's obvious that you don't want it so we'll forget the boat trip,' she said. 'We'll just walk along the river bank and you can—'

'No!' He pointed back the way they had come. 'We'll walk up a hill somewhere. Find a quiet bit of the Delamere Forest.'

'And we'll talk there?'

'If you wish,' he said.

She drove for a quarter of an hour in silence. From time to time she glanced at him but there was no way she could read his expression. So she felt fearful. It had been a brilliant idea. What had gone wrong? She clenched her teeth. Whatever it was, she could deal with it.

In time they found a deserted car park, a path ran from it up a hill. They started to walk. Very deliberately she took his hand, held it tight. He squeezed back. Well, that was a start.

At the top of the hill there was a tree trunk to sit on, a view over miles of the Cheshire plain. She remembered how he had liked the view from the top of the Pennines. This should suit him, too.

They sat side by side; she put her arm round his shoulders for a moment. 'Now, tell me,' she said.

'In fact, I was going to. Going to tell you today. Last Tuesday you told me all about yourself, and I wanted to do the same for you. I wanted to wait until my birthday and then we could laugh about things together.'

'You don't sound as if you're in a laughing mood.'

'Just the prospect of a trip by water put me off a little.' He took a deep breath. 'Miranda, remember I once told you that I'd been...entangled?'

'I remember it very well.'

'Well, it was the biggest mistake I've ever made or intend to make. I was more than entangled. I was married.'

This shocked her; she looked at him wide-eyed. 'I should have known that. Not that it makes any difference to us, but I should have been told.'

He took her hand. 'I'm sorry, sweetheart. Nobody else in the hospital knows except Toby and Carly and they know how I feel about it. How I want it kept secret.'

He sighed. 'I suppose that's why I'm not as...affable as I could be. I thought that if I kept people at a distance then I wouldn't get...entangled again.'

'You mean hurt. So tell me about it.'

He lifted her hand to his lips, kissed her knuckles abstractedly. 'Well, the comic bit first. My marriage came to an unfortunate end on a boat trip. On the Thames, in fact. And it was on my birthday.'

Miranda winced. 'And I thought that whatever I liked you'd like, too. Made a mess of things, didn't I?'

'You weren't to know. It was eight years ago today. I was a senior registrar in London, working on the neonatal unit and working all the hours that God sent. I'd just been offered a job here at the Dell Owen and I was looking forward to moving up to where I came from. I'd been married to Veronica for three years. She was a doctor, too, younger than me—in fact, she was still an SHO. Like a lot of medical people in those days, we were working so hard that we had a bit of a hurried wedding. Quick service, a few friends round, no honeymoon, straight back to work again.'

'I've been to a few of those,' Miranda said.

'Well, if I ever get married again, I want the full Monty. I want all my friends and family, a formal suit, a bride in a full-length white dress, a church with a choir and then a honeymoon. Miranda, a wedding should be something to celebrate!'

'I agree.' Miranda's voice was choked. She felt uneasy but she managed to hide her doubts. But there was one thing she had to ask. After a moment's silence, 'What did Veronica look like?'

'Very small, very slim, blonde hair. Always perfectly dressed, perfectly made-up. She wouldn't go out until she looked immaculate.'

'Right,' said Miranda. 'The opposite of me. So you're attracted to me because I'm a scruff?'

He smiled, leaned over to kiss her cheek. 'Among other reasons,' he said. 'Anyway, Veronica came from a wealthy family who lived in London. I'm not sure how she felt about moving out of her posh house into my rather cramped little flat.'

Miranda felt that she'd have been more than happy to move into a hovel with Jack. But she said nothing.

Jack went on, 'I got this job at the Dell Owen. I was going to buy a biggish house and I thought we'd agreed to start a family. And I thought Veronica agreed. But we were both very busy and we didn't seem to see much of each other.

'Anyway, there was a big hospital party on a boat cruising up the Thames. There were a lot of parties like that. There was a bit of dancing, a lot of drinking. Veronica got drunk and she was making a bit of a show of herself, dancing with a consultant quite a bit older than her. I tried to tell her she was making a fool of herself. You know I hate scenes. But we had a big row on the boat. She screamed that she was leaving me, she apparently had been sleeping with the consultant for months. No way was she going up north. And the thought of having babies with me made her feel sick. I went to talk to the consultant and he must have thought I was going to kill him.'

Jack smiled bitterly. 'Not so. I was going to tell him that he could have Veronica with pleasure. And then—just to make things even more farcical—he jumped overboard. To get away from me. Imagine the gossip that caused. And I had to stay in the job for another three months.'

Jack stared up at the steel-blue sky for a moment. 'And since that time I've kept people at a distance. Kept my working life very separate from my private life. Until I met you.'

'What a birthday present I got you,' Miranda said forlornly. 'I couldn't have picked worse if I tried. Jack, I'm so sorry.'

His arm was already round her, he squeezed her and then kissed her. 'That boat goes regularly, doesn't it?' he asked. 'When's the next trip?'

'What?'

'We've told each other everything now. The past is behind us. And I always liked water. Let's go on the trip you promised me.'

'What…? But you'll feel…'

'I'll feel my past is dead and I'm with you,' he said. 'Now I have a future.'

'I think there's another trip in twenty minutes,' she said.

It was only a small operation, the repair of an inguinal hernia in a tiny boy. Some of his intestines protruded through the wall of his abdomen and would have to be eased back and the pouch they had made removed. Quite a simple operation. Miranda had worked an early shift that morning; this was the afternoon. Jack had said that if she wanted, she could observe again. Of course she wanted to observe. She loved the atmosphere in the theatre.

But this time was going to be different. After she had scrubbed up, Jack came over and said, 'A change of plan. You're going to be scrub nurse for me to get some training.'

'But what…? But I… What about Charlotte?'

'Charlotte is going to sit by and watch. If need be, she'll correct you. But you're the official one in charge.'

'I don't know half as much as Charlotte!'

'I should hope not, she's been doing it for years. You'll be slower, you might get things wrong. But the surgeon in charge is willing to make allowances.'

'I wonder why.'

So she was scrub nurse. And she thought she did…well, not brilliantly but adequately.

'You'll be good in time,' Jack told her afterwards, and she decided to take this as high praise.

She went home with him that night—these days she often did. And she cooked for him. Working in his kitchen was like being captain of a starship; there were so many knobs, controls, dials. But she learned. And she loved cooking there.

'That was a wonderful meal,' he said lazily after they had eaten. 'That beef stew and those baked vegetables were superb. Did you cook them or does that kitchen do them all for you?'

'That kitchen needs an expert cook like me!' She sniffed. 'And it wasn't a beef stew, it was a beef daube.'

'Sorry. What's the difference?'

'I'm not sure. Different pages of the cookery book.'

They were in his living room, sitting on the couch. He was sitting at one end with his legs stretched along its length and she was sitting between his legs, her back leaning against his chest. His arms were round her, his lips nuzzling her hair. She felt happy, complete.

'There's something I want to say to you,' he went on.

His voice appeared quite normal but he didn't speak for a while. So, sleepily, she said, 'What do you want to say to me, then?'

'I think that I love you.'

She tensed, twisted round in his arms to stare at him. 'What did you say?'

'I said I think that I love you. That's a bit feeble. I know I'm awkward at this kind of thing. For years I was used to keeping my emotions well hidden. You've taught me how to show them. You almost blackmailed me into showing them. But now I'm glad. And I think I'm sure I love you.' He looked faintly puzzled, as if surprised at what he had just said.

Miranda felt equally surprised. This was the last thing she had been expecting. She felt there ought to have been some kind of build-up to a declaration like this, some kind of indication as to the way he was thinking. Not just a statement out of the blue.

Quickly following this feeling came another. He loved her! He'd said so; it was the first time! And a joy she had never felt before rushed through her. He loved her! But the joy was quickly replaced by desolation.

She put a finger over his mouth. 'Don't say any more, Jack. Don't rush things. We agreed to take time to get to know each other, to take one day at a time.'

'I'm tired of taking one day at a time. I want to—'

'I know what you're going to say. But, Jack, remember! I can't have children.' Now the desolation was disappearing and in its place came a horror. She had been happy in her life with Jack, getting to know him, enjoying his company, sleeping with him. They had decided, for a while, to ignore the future. But now that future was here and it had to be dealt with.

'Jack, I tried not to let this happen. We can only have nowhere is no future for us. One stark fact. I can't have babies. And you need them.'

'I need you, Miranda! I can't imagine life without you now. Do you know how much I love you?'

She burst into tears. 'You can't,' she wept. 'Now what are we going to do?'

He pulled her head onto his shoulder, stroked her hair. 'We're going to carry on as we were before,' he said. 'We're going to get to know each other see as much of each other as we possibly can. So far in my life I've never put my happiness into the hands of someone else. But you I know I can trust.'

Then there came into his voice just a hint of the old, certain Jack. The man who was going to get his own way or there'd be trouble. 'Just two things different. One, now you know for certain that I love you. Two, we have a future together. Right?'

She managed a smile through the tears. 'Right, Jack,' she said.

If he was upset at not hearing that she loved him, he didn't show it. So she said nothing more. She couldn't raise his hopes.

It was to be a day of surprises. She was working on the ward when Jack grabbed her, kissed her quickly because no one was looking. 'Things are changing,' he said. 'First of all, I'm going to Barcelona early tomorrow. Two days in a conference and then for ten days I'm going to work in a local hospital with a couple of Spanish surgeons. We've got ideas we want to exchange. But when I get back I'll need, and I'll be entitled to, a holiday. I want you to book some time off, five days should do. Little country girl, we'll fly to the metropolis and look at the sights. We'll go to London. Get away from constant work and pressure. And since we'll have plenty of time, we can think about our future.'

'Our future?'

'Yes. We need to—'

'Mr Sinclair, we've got a bit of a problem with Baby Nelson and we'd like you to have a look.' A rather scared-looking young nurse had appeared.

'Be right there, Rebecca.' Jack looked at Miranda. 'Work calls. See you later.' Then he was walking away.

In fact, he didn't see her later. There was a message on her phone—he was needed at the hospital, would sleep there and go straight to the airport in the morning. Not to forget to book the time off for when he came back. Oh, and he loved her.

Miranda sighed. She had some thinking to do.

Later that night she lay in her own bed and felt lonely. There was something about sharing a bed with a man that you loved. Not just the passion, though that was wonderful, it was the togetherness. The warmth of his body when he was asleep. The rhythm of his breathing. The drowsy smile he gave her first thing in the morning.

He was going away for a few days and when he came back they were going to London. It would be their first ever holiday together. He had said they'd get away from constant work and pressure and think about their future. She suspected she knew what that would mean. He would ask her to marry him.

She desperately wanted to marry him.

But she couldn't give him babies. And of all the men she had ever met, she knew that Jack was the one who most needed to have a child of his own.

She knew he would say that it didn't matter she couldn't have babies, it was her that he loved. And he'd mean it. But in time she was sure that he'd come to feel the loss more and more. Perhaps even resent her...

What could she do? The good, the strong thing to do might be to leave him. Tell him to find some other woman. But even as she thought about it, she knew she wouldn't have the strength. And he wouldn't let her walk away from him. He was Jack Sinclair, he knew exactly what he meant to her.

What could she do? Her brain was going round and round. It was a pointless exercise. There was no solution and she was driving herself mad.

And just as her wearied brain could take no more, and she was dropping off into a fitful sleep, the vaguest of thoughts slipped into her mind.

What about America?

CHAPTER EIGHT

SHE had to do it while she still had the courage.

Next day she got into work early, checked the rosters. Annoyingly, Carly had the day off. But there was a list of home numbers in the office, so Miranda phoned her.

'Carly? It's Miranda. Are you at home all day?'

'A rare day off,' agreed a cheerful voice. 'I shall spend it sleeping and studying. What can I do for you?'

'Could I call round after my shift?'

'It would be great to see you. You can look at my tiny home. Is there any special reason why—?'

'Got to go. See you then,' said Miranda, and rang off. She had done it now, there was no turning back.

Carly had leased a small one-bedroomed flat for a year. Miranda stood outside the block, looking at the new bricks and paintwork. Under her arm was a red plastic folder, which she'd carried to work that morning.

She could still turn back, of course. No, she couldn't. She rang Carly's bell.

Carly seemed pleased to see her, 'Hi, sis,' she greeted merrily.

Miranda blinked. 'Sis?'

Carly grinned. 'I've always wanted one. Two brothers, one girl, it's not good enough. Who can I have girlish chats with? Now, I've got the tea things laid out in the kitchen, I'll make us some tea in a minute. Sit down on the couch.'

She looked thoughtfully at Miranda. 'You've got a look,' she said. 'I've seen it on mothers sometimes when they're about to give birth for the first time. A combination of determination and fear. And if you're here, it must be about big brother.'

She grinned again. 'Not pregnant, are you?'

Miranda bit her lip, tried to keep the hurt out of her eyes. She saw the smile fade on Carly's face. 'I've said the wrong thing, haven't I, Miranda? God, I'm so sorry. Come on, tell me what it is. You're not really pregnant, are you?'

Miranda offered her the folder. 'I'll make the tea,' she said. 'You be a doctor and read this.'

When Miranda returned with the tray of tea, Carly just nodded and carried on reading. Miranda didn't mind; she recognised this switching-off technique. She'd seen it in Jack sometimes. Concentrate on the facts. Once you'd mastered them you could think about the emotional implications.

In the back of the folder was a set of X-rays. Carly took them out, held them up to the light and pursed her lips. Just as Miranda had seen Jack do. She drank her tea at the same time.

Carly got to the end of the folder, turned back and looked up a couple of details. Then she looked at

Miranda with that assessing look that Miranda had seen doctors give patients before. 'An interesting case,' she said. 'You were lucky to survive.'

'I suppose so,' said Miranda.

'But you've made a very good recovery.'

'Parts of me have. Carly, could...? Is it possible...? This new technique you've been working on in Chicago. The microsurgery. Could it work on the bits of me that were damaged? Could they be repaired so I could have babies again?'

Carly looked shocked. 'Oh, Miranda. Is that what you want?'

'Definitely,' Miranda replied staunchly.

Carly sighed at the determined expression on her friend's face and ran a hand through her straight, dark hair, her grey eyes full of concern. 'Well, you know it's experimental, it's dangerous, it's expensive,' she said. 'Let me expand. We don't know the long-term prognosis. Whatever good is done might just disappear. And it doesn't always work. So far it's about fifty-fifty, with some people it's successful, with others it isn't. And we don't know why. One poor lady was left in a wheelchair as a result. And in no way do you get it done for free. This procedure would be in the USA, it's not available in the UK. Though I hope in a few years that the technique might come back to this country with me.'

'I got thirty thousand pounds in damages after the crash,' Miranda said. 'I've never touched it. I'll happily spend the lot on this operation.'

'The risk? The chance of the rest of your life in a wheelchair?'

'I'll take the chance. Remember Jenny Donovan? She was in a wheelchair, she's getting about now.'

Carly considered. 'I'm supposed to counsel you but I'm not quite sure how to do it. What does Jack say about this?'

'He doesn't know and I'm not going to ask him or tell him. This is my decision.'

'What? But the two of you are—?'

'Yes we are. But it's still my decision.'

Carly winced. 'You know he's a surgeon, he cuts babies—people—open for a living. But he's never more happy than when he can say it's not necessary. He doesn't like being invasive. And another thing. Whatever is being decided, he likes to be consulted.'

'I know that, too. I don't want to argue with him.'

Carly looked apprehensive. 'Think what he'll say to me when he thinks I've gone behind his back.' Then she smiled. 'Got a pound coin?'

Curious, Miranda found one in her purse, handed it over.

'Now you've paid me and I'm your doctor. Patient confidentiality and all that. This is a consultation.' Then she was serious again. 'Miranda, I think you should tell him.'

'I know what he'd say.' Miranda was definite. 'He'd say that it wasn't worth the risk and I was just doing it for him and that I wasn't to. Well, he's wrong. I'm doing it for me. So will you help me?'

Carly stared at her for a moment. Then she reached

for her phone. 'It's morning in Chicago now,' she said. 'I'll phone my old professor.'

Miranda met Carly again the next day. They sat in Carly's flat again, drank more tea.

'What did your old professor say?' Miranda asked eagerly.

'We'll come to that bit in a minute,' Carly said. 'There's other things to be considered first.' She reached for the red folder, flipped it open and studied a page. 'Remember what you felt like when you were in hospital?'

'I remember. The staff were great, I was one of their own, but I never want to go through anything like that again. The pain and the discomfort and the nurses and doctors messing me about—I hated it. And I'd lost the man I was going to marry. I thought I'd never cope.'

'But you're willing to go through all that again? Even though it might be unsuccessful?'

'Yes,' said Miranda.

Carly flipped further through the red folder. 'I have to tell you that I faxed copies of this folder to my professor and he's not too keen on performing the operation. The odds aren't good. Your surgeon had to cut perilously near the sciatic nerve. You know what would have happened if there'd been much trouble there?'

'Paraplegia? Lower half of the body paralysed?'

'Exactly. If you have this new operation, you'll be risking that again.'

Miranda scowled at her friend. 'I know what you're trying to do and it's no good. If there's any chance, I want that operation!'

Carefully, Carly put away the sheet she had been holding. 'There's a good chance that you'll come home from this operation in a wheelchair. Jack will get out of you what you've done—and he'll know why. Then he'll insist on marrying you because—'

'Carly! I want that operation! If he asked me right now to marry him, I wouldn't. Because he needs to have babies. And let me guarantee you one thing. If I come home in a wheelchair, I will *not* marry your brother. No matter how many times he gets on his bended knee.'

'That I would like to see,' muttered Carly. 'OK, Miranda, I've been as clear as I can. If it was me, I wouldn't have this operation. But it's your choice.' To Miranda's surprise Carly came over and kissed her. 'I hope my brother realises how lucky he is.'

Even though Miranda was a bank nurse and not required to give notice, the next morning she went to see Jenny Donovan. 'Jenny, I wanted you to know what's happening,' she said. 'I have to leave for a while. But I've loved working here and I would like to come back. I'd love to have a job here, too, if that was possible.'

Jenny looked at her calmly. 'We want you on the staff here, for all sorts of reasons. Do you want to tell me why you are going?'

Miranda was blunt. 'I'm going to America for an operation that might make me capable of having children again.'

She could tell Jenny was shocked at that, but she hid it well. 'You've thought hard about it, measured up the chances and so on?'

'Yes, I have.'

'Good.' Jenny looked at her thoughtfully. 'You look a bit tired,' she said.

'I was awake all night, wondering and worrying. I've got to do this now or I'll never do it.'

'What does Jack think about it?'

'Jenny! This is my body! I make the decisions about it.'

'Is there anything I can do to persuade you to at least talk to him?'

Miranda's shoulders slumped. 'I know what he'd say. He'd try to talk me out of it and I'm afraid I'd give in. Jenny, I need this chance.'

Jenny looked at her in silence for a minute, then apparently made up her mind about something. 'Then good luck. And keep us all posted. We all think a lot of you here, Miranda.'

Two days later, three days after Jack had left, Miranda boarded a plane at Manchester airport, bound for Chicago. Carly, Annie and Jenny were the only three people who knew where or why she was going.

Miranda winced when she saw the facilities that were available in the Chicago Dana Hospital. The car park was vast, the building was sparkling, the staff efficient and pleasant. Inside, every possible medical or surgical need was catered for—in abundance. Money appeared to be no object.

But she soon found out why. Most of her money was disappearing—a little had gone on the air fare, the rest on medical expenses. Fortunately, Carly had done some negotiating for her. She had got her a guaranteed price for the operation and all possible eventualities. And she had found her a discount. But still it made Miranda heartily thankful for the NHS.

She liked Larry Laker, Carly's old professor, the surgeon who was pioneering the treatment. A genial man in his late fifties, with half-moon glasses and a mane of white hair, he looked just like a television surgeon. But under the amiable exterior she could tell there was an incisive mind.

'If you had been working for me for a while,' he said, 'I could have arranged a really large discount. Do you fancy working in the USA?'

'It's an interesting idea,' she muttered, 'but I'll see what it's like from the patient's side first.'

'An interesting idea! Every doctor should be a patient sometimes. It would give some of them a shock. Now, are you ready to start this afternoon?'

It began here. 'As soon as possible.'

'Good. There's a whole battery of tests, scans, X-rays, investigations that we need to get out of the way first. It'll be uncomfortable and undignified, but I know you know about things like that. Then I'll have a good look at the results and come and have a word with you again. I hope we can do well for you, Miranda!'

So she had the tests. They seemed to happen incredibly quickly, and the results came back in hours instead of—as some of them did in the UK—in days. And then Professor Laker came to her bedside with a large pad and a pencil.

'We could start tomorrow morning,' he said. 'You'll be prepped and then I'll see you in Theatre. Now, I'm a firm believer that people should know what's happening to them. And medical people especially. And I like to know my patients. I have this foolish feeling that if the person under the knife is known to me as a person, not just a case, then I'll operate better.'

Miranda was interested in this. 'I've known surgeons who think exactly the opposite. That they work better if they're…passionless?'

'No surgeon is passionless, it's just that some hide it well. I like to chat to my patients. But each to what suits him. Now, I've read your notes, I've checked and double-checked all the investigations we've made. I know Carly Sinclair has spoken to you. And I've got to tell you this, Miranda. This operation is a risk that I normally would not take. There is a chance we might be able to put things right for you. But there's a chance we can do very little. And there's a definite chance you'll finish up a paraplegic.'

Somehow, now it all seemed more real. And perhaps for the first time Miranda faced up to what could happen to her. The rest of her life in a wheelchair? But she had come so far. 'I know that,' she said. 'It's a risk I'm prepared to take.'

'You know I'm going to ask you to sign a release form—in effect, you sign your life away. I'm going far too close to the sciatic nerve to be comfortable, your lower limbs could be paralysed.' He looked weary. 'One of my patients still is in a wheelchair. And I'm not sure that I know why.'

'I trust you and I'm willing to take a chance.'

'Do you mind telling me why?'

Miranda liked this man and didn't mind confiding in him. 'I believe that the man I hope to marry will only be fully complete, fully happy if he can see a child of his own.'

'Has he said so? Sent you to have this operation?'

'He doesn't even know I'm here,' Miranda told him.

'But surely he should at least be consulted?' The professor was obviously surprised.

'Some decisions are best made by just one person.'

The professor nodded. 'Perhaps. Well, whoever he is, he must be one amazing person for you to go through with this. He's a lucky man, and I hope he'll still be lucky when the operation is over. OK, see you in Theatre tomorrow morning.'

'When…when will I know if the operation is successful?'

'We'll have a reasonably good idea after forty-eight hours,' he said.

* * *

Next morning she should have been nervous; she seemed to be so far away from friends. But it didn't feel that way. The decision she had made, the chance she was taking—it was all so great that she distanced herself from it. It was done now. All she had to do was lie there and hope.

She was prepped, a trocar slid into the vein in the back of her hand. Then a smiling anaesthetist came to bend over her, make a last check. She knew that she...

The anaesthetic hadn't worked. She felt fuzzy but still awake, she'd better tell someone. 'I'm still awake,' she grumbled to a vague white-coated figure. 'I need another dose.'

'Honey, it worked all right. The operation is all over. You're done.'

'Oh,' said Miranda, and went back to sleep.

Some time later she woke up again. Sort of woke up, and she decided that being asleep was much better. She didn't really know what was happening. She had a headache, her mouth tasted terrible, her sight was still bleary and there was a pain down below.

And sitting by her bed was Jack.

Jack?

She blinked several times then screwed up her eyes tight. When she opened them he was still there. She tried to remember. She was in Chicago and had just had an operation; he was in Barcelona. This must be some kind of hallucination. Her fuzzy brain was seeing things that were impossible. But when she reached out a tentative hand, she could feel his arm, his sleeve. A pretty solid hallucination.

'Jack? What are you doing here?'

'I've come to see you. How are you?'

'I feel terrible. I'm fine.' It was a struggle to get her thoughts together. Jack shouldn't be here, she was going to tell him about it afterwards when... 'Jack, has it been a success?'

'I don't know. I'm not sure what's happening.' Even in her vague state she could tell there was a touch of harshness in his voice. 'I've not been consulted, have I?'

A nurse came over. 'I think that's enough now, sir. The patient needs rest. If you could wait outside.'

'Can't I sit here with her and just keep quiet?'

'She won't rest if she knows you're here, and she needs sleep.' There was a pause and then Miranda heard the nurse go on, 'And if you don't mind my saying so, sir, you look as if you could do with a rest yourself.'

'Right. Thank you, Nurse.' Miranda felt him lean over her, kiss her on the forehead. Then he was gone.

Miranda was still very sleepy. But she felt that Jack seemed less than overjoyed to be with her. Still...sleep now.

It was two hours later when Miranda woke up again, and she felt more alert now. She was also in considerably more pain. But she had expected that.

Professor Laker was looking down at her, his face thoughtful. 'How do you feel Miranda? Need a pain-killer?'

Well, yes, now she was awake, she realised she did. The pain was there and it was growing by the minute.

But there were things she had to know first, she could hold on a bit longer. 'The pain is there but I can stand it for a while. Professor Laker, was the operation a success?' She could hear the anxiety in her own voice.

'Wriggle your toes. Can you feel them?'

She did as he said. 'My toes seem fine. Is that a good thing?'

'Well, it means that you won't be in a wheelchair. In fact, I didn't have to go anywhere near the sciatic nerve.'

He took a chair, drew it to the side of her bed. He was closer now and she saw the strain lines round his eyes and mouth, heard the weariness in his voice. He was exhausted.

'Miranda, you were a mess inside. The surgeon who dealt with you before did a very fine job, but his first priority was just to keep you alive, not to ensure that some day you might have babies. And he wasn't a microsurgeon like me, he didn't have my training, my tools, my technicians. In effect, I had to fit together the parts that he had discarded. And I don't mind telling you, I'm rather proud of myself. Yours was the worst case I've ever dealt with.'

'So I can have babies now?'

Professor Laker looked cautious. 'Possibly. Or even possibly-probably. Miranda, I took two hours longer than I normally do. I sewed together tubes that had openings the size of a human hair. No matter how desperately I try, there's always the chance of a kink or a blockage. But I am optimistic. We'll be examining you at regular intervals, of course, and in your case I want to wait four days before I go to have a closer look. Let things settle down a little. After that, I'll be able to give you a much clearer idea.'

Miranda was a professional, she knew what the professor was doing. If parents asked you about the health of their children, you always had to be honest. If a condition was life-threatening, they had to be told. Nothing was more cruel than false hope. So the professor was indicating that things could go either way. Well, she could live with that. For four days. Just live with it.

She must be waking up more. Pain flashed through her body and she squeezed her eyes shut and tried to stop herself moaning. It felt as if the whole of the lower half of her body was on fire.

Her surgeon had, of course, noticed her sudden agony. 'I'm giving you something to make you sleep now,' he said. Moments late she felt a prick in her arm. Then he went on, 'Now, I don't want you getting excited but I gather you had a visitor earlier. Jack Sinclair, a neonatal surgeon. I've suggested to him that it might be a good idea if he didn't see you again till tomorrow, you'll be awake then. How he got here I don't know. But we've had a few words and I'm having dinner with him tonight. We have a lot in common.'

Miranda bit her lip. 'Will you tell him that I—?'

He held up his hand. 'I will absolutely refuse to discuss your case except to say that I think you're out of danger.'

Now the painkiller was acting, Miranda felt a sense of peace, as if she were swimming through warm water. She managed to mumble, 'You can tell him everything. I want him to know.'

'Then you must be the one to tell him,' Professor Laker said.

But Miranda was asleep.

She had a reasonable night and when she woke up next morning she felt a lot more alert, but still in a lot more pain. Well. she had invited it and she was content. She knew the morning nursing procedure in a gynae ward, she had followed it herself so often. But it was odd, seeing it from the patient's rather than from the nurse's side. And there were differences in protocol between American and British nursing.

She felt subdued, not really emotional at all. She had taken a gamble, it would be three days more before she knew if the gamble had paid off. And she didn't really care what the outcome was. She could wait and see.

Of course, she knew that this reaction was partly due to the anaesthetic she had been given, the drugs she was taking. But she was content to wait and see. There was nothing else to do.

But what about Jack? How had he got there? She had to confess to being a little apprehensive about Jack.

After the obs, drug round, breakfast and washing, she felt better. 'You have a visitor,' the nurse told her. 'But only for five minutes.'

It must be Jack. Miranda felt just a touch wary, there were things to explain. She hoped he realised this had all been done for him.

He came to sit by her bed and her heart thumped when she saw him. He was dressed as the old cool

Jack—dark suit, white shirt and club tie. Probably a good idea to dress to impress, she thought.

'How are you feeling Miranda?'

'I can think straight now. There's some pain. Never again will I tell a patient not to bother about the pain, that it'll go in time. But I'm OK.'

She looked at him, the old Jack, stern and unsmiling. 'You can kiss me, you know,' she said. 'Just gently on the cheek.'

So he did. And while he was close she could feel him, smell that mixture of aftershave and warmth that was uniquely, excitingly Jack. Her heart filled with emotion. But for the moment there was little she could say.

'What are you doing here? You were supposed to be in Barcelona, not Chicago.'

'I went to the conference. The visit to the hospital afterwards was cancelled. I'll have to go back in a month or so. Anyway, I came back to England and everyone was vague about where you were. I knew something was being kept from me and I didn't like it.'

'I'm sorry,' Miranda said.

'Jenny got all professional on me, said she couldn't discuss it, but that I should have faith in you. Annie wouldn't talk about you but said I should trust you. When I said you should trust me, she said I didn't deserve you. So I got angry.'

Miranda felt miserable. 'I didn't want all this,' she said.

'Neither did I. Then Toby told me, quite casually, that he'd seen you going to Carly's flat with a red folder under your arm. I remembered that folder, I knew what was in it. Carly wouldn't tell me anything, but when she mentioned her old professor, I guessed. This is her old hospital. I phoned and found out you were here and I flew straight out.'

'You don't sound very happy,' Miranda said.

'I'm not. I've always gone my own way, made decisions myself. Then I met you and things seemed to change. I wanted to share everything with you. And then you did something that... Miranda, all operations are a risk.'

When she looked at him she realised just how worried he had been. Still...

'But I did it for you!'

'Perhaps you did. But if you had—'

There was a knock on the door and a nurse entered. 'Sorry, sir, time for dressings. You'll have to leave now. And then this patient needs rest.'

Miranda noticed the appreciative way the nurse eyed Jack's tall figure and well-cut suit. But she was also going to do her job.

Jack stood, frowning.

'You can kiss me again before you go,' said Miranda. So he kissed her and then he went.

After the dressings, when the nurse had gone, Miranda laid her head on the pillow and cried. What was wrong with him?

Things got worse. Professor Laker came in, not to examine her but, as he said, to have a friendly chat. He said that if she made good progress and if she made sure that she took thing very easy, then perhaps she could fly home in ten days.

'I'll refer you to a gynae consultant, John Bennett. I gather you know him. And I'll phone him and have a word. Now, while you are here we'll keep a steady eye on you and we're going to keep you quiet. And when you get home, let me make something clear. You are not to go straight back to work. You are to take things very easy. The work I have done inside you will take quite some time to settle down. OK?'

'OK,' said Miranda.

'Jack Sinclair's a very bright man, very impressive. You couldn't persuade him to come and work over here?'

'I couldn't persuade him to do anything he doesn't want to do,' Miranda said gloomily.

'I can imagine. I'm sorry I shan't be seeing him again.'

'What?'

Professor Laker looked rather upset. 'He's gone back to England. It was a flying visit to see you, he must be very fond of you. He asked me to give you this letter. Now, like I said, take it easy and I'll be in to see you tomorrow.' He patted her hand and left.

Miranda waited a few minutes, the white envelope lying unopened on her bed. Jack had left? A letter, no visit to say goodbye? All this way and then rush back? Exactly what did she mean to him?

She opened the letter.

Dear Miranda,
I'm writing this before I leave for the airport. I

have to get the first possible plane back. I'm
needed desperately in the UK as four neonatal
surgeons are off sick. I'm the handiest replace-
ment so I'm going. Let me know when you're
coming back and I'll meet you. We can talk then.
Regards, Jack

She re-read the letter, looked at it in despair.
Regards, Jack! What was wrong with *Love, Jack? Can
talk?* She didn't want to talk. What about their trip to
London, the promise that things would change? She'd
show him change!

Of course, she knew that he was right about having
to fly back. There was a shortage of neonatal surgeons.
But he could have done better with his note. *Regards!*
She'd show him!

She was surprised to find that she was angry.

And she still didn't know if the operation had been
a success.

CHAPTER NINE

IN SOME ways it was a relief for Jack to do what he knew he did best. He stood by the table, masked and gowned, surrounded by his team. He was the team leader, completely in control. The team had been trained to know, to anticipate, exactly what he wanted.

Usually it only took him a couple of seconds to focus. Today it was a bit more difficult. Was it because he was still jet-lagged? Or was it because of Miranda? What should he do about her?

He realised that he was waiting longer than usual and the anaesthetist was looking at him, apparently rather surprised. That decided him. A mammoth effort of will and he bent to his task. All thoughts about anything other than the operation in question were banished.

It was like that for the rest of his day. He couldn't keep his mind fixed on what he had to do—the consultations with his SHOs, the round to check that all was well, the never-ending paperwork. And because he was conscious that he wasn't concentrating, everything had to be checked twice. He couldn't afford a mistake. And this made his work last longer and made him even more angry.

He was even more lost when his day's work ended. Usually he found his flat a peaceful refuge from the turmoil of work. Not this evening. He looked at his pictures, ran his fingers over his Lalique glassware, stared at the swirling colours on his rug. None of the beautiful things he had surrounded himself with could give him any peace.

He went to his study, checked his telephone. There were a dozen messages, none of them of any great importance. Then there was one from Miranda.

Her voice was hesitant, weak, and he could hardly stand the conflicting emotions it raised inside him. 'This is just to say that it was lovely of you to come out all the way to see me. I do understand that you had to go back but I would have liked you to stay.' There was a long pause and then she went on, 'I think I'm still under the effect of the surgery and the anaesthetic. I'm not sure what I'm feeling or thinking. But I miss you. Goodbye.'

He played the message twice more to try to get the last bit of meaning out of it. She was not sure what she was thinking or feeling. Well, neither was he. He just couldn't understand his feelings about Miranda.

He wasn't happy. He knew that what she had done she had done for him. But they had agreed that they would share everything—especially decisions! And then she had taken the most important decision he could imagine without even mentioning it to him.

It had been painful for him to change the attitudes of most of his lifetime. He now realised that he had never been really close to Veronica—and he had been married to her! And after they had parted he had decided to keep to himself, keep his own counsel, be wary of other people. That way you didn't get let down. Didn't leave yourself open to hurt and gossip. He had thought Miranda was different and he had tried to share with her, though at times it was hard. She'd never told him she loved him. Then she had set off on her own. Perhaps he had been wrong about her. Perhaps he'd been happier as the cold, distant consultant.

Ten minutes later his mobile rang, the number only a few people knew. It was Carly. She sounded surprised.

'What are you doing back here, Jack? I thought you'd gone to Chicago.'

'I was called back. Emergencies.'

Carly knew how stretched the neonatal surgeons were. 'I might have guessed. Did you see Miranda?'

'I did.'

'Was the operation a success?'

'They're not sure yet. But so far things are looking reasonable.'

'Big brother, why are you sounding so irritable? Do you know what she's done? Do you know she's done it for you?'

'I know that but I…'

'But you what?'

'This was a decision we should have taken together.'

'So you felt left out. How terrible.'

His sister was obviously getting angry. That interested him. Usually she didn't dare shout at him.

'Jack, first of all it's her body, she makes the decisions. Second, she did it to spare you the guilt if things went wrong. Only she could take that decision. Third, she did it because she loves you. Sometimes, Jack Sinclair, you can be so thick!'

Carly rang off. Not a good phone call, Jack thought. He was too gloomy to get angry with her.

Miranda had thought that if she was careful, she'd be all right travelling back home the way she had come. But Professor Laker wouldn't hear of it. 'You're not going to undo all my good work by fighting your way across the Atlantic,' he said. 'I'll make a couple of phone calls.' And so a taxi took her to the airport and she was met there by a courteous man pushing a wheelchair. 'I can walk slowly...' she started, but her case was taken from her, she was eased into the wheelchair, taken quickly through customs, immigration and so on and was first onto the plane. She was given a seat with plenty of leg room. Another man with a wheelchair met her in Manchester. It was all too easy.

And now she was being pushed towards Jack.

She saw him waiting for her and, as ever, felt that thump of excitement. Obviously he had come straight from the hospital. He was wearing the dark suit and a pure white shirt. Was that a bad sign? Was the old Jack resurfacing? She didn't know.

It had been quite a while since she had spoken to him.

They both could have worked harder at getting in touch by phone, but had contented themselves with leaving messages. She wasn't sure how they would treat each other. She wasn't sure what barrier had come between them. Perhaps, on her part, it was just the after-effects of a long and difficult operation. She knew from experience that sometimes patients had mental as well as physical reactions to the stress of being under an anaesthetic and having major surgery.

But he smiled, kissed her and took the bag she carried on her lap. 'It's good to have you back,' he said. 'I won't hug you, I don't want to disturb things. My car is very close.'

She felt that lack of communication that sometimes came to people who wanted to be close, but couldn't. 'You can't go back to work for quite a while,' he said. 'John Bennett told me that.'

'I'll take things easy. I'm not going to risk anything until I get the all-clear.'

'Good. Incidentally, everyone's been asking after you, you're very popular. The most frequent rumour is that you've had a minor surgical problem.'

'Very minor,' she said.

After leaving the airport, they drove for a while in silence. She looked at his hard profile, remembered how she had once thought it craggy. Well, it was craggy. But it was also wonderful.

It was almost as if he had read her mind. Suddenly he smiled, and as always his face was transformed. And his body seemed to relax. He felt for her hand, squeezed it, then let go to drive. 'It's so good to see you well,' he said, 'but do you know what you've put me through? I worry, Miranda.'

'I did it for you, Jack. No, I did it for us.'

'I guessed. Now, this is a bit forward of me, but since you've got to take things easy, I thought you might like to stay for a while in my flat.'

'What?'

'Well, Annie is very happy for you to go back to the flat you share, but the bedroom is tiny, the bed even tinier. At my place you can spread yourself out a bit.'

'You told Annie I was going to stay at your flat?'

For a moment there was the old Jack. 'It makes more sense,' he said curtly. 'You've had a serious operation, you need rest to recover quickly. You will be more comfortable in my spare bedroom than in your own.'

Then, perhaps, he heard himself because he said in a softer voice, 'And I would very much like it if you stayed with me.'

She thought for a moment. 'Yes, I think I'd like that, too,' she said.

It seemed strange to be driving back into Liverpool, seeing familiar surroundings as they drove off the motorway. She'd only been away for a few days, but things seemed to have changed. Or perhaps she had changed. At his flat, she walked slowly upstairs as he carried her bag. He took her to the spare bedroom. The spare bedroom?

'You always feel sticky after a long plane flight,' he said. 'Why don't you have a shower? I've put out towels, there's everything you should need. And you must be hungry but for now I'll just do tea and sandwiches. Come along when you're ready.'

And he left her.

Miranda had a shower and it made her feel better. She felt a bit hungry. But most of all she felt angry. What was wrong with the man? He was treating her like his sister, she thought. Well, she'd had enough of it.

Although it was very early evening, she put on a dressing-gown. A very smart one. Then she took a little care of her hair and put on a touch of make-up. She was not his patient, she was his lover! She was not an invalid. She walked along the corridor ready to do battle.

One thing about having an ankle-length gown, you could swish in a very satisfactory manner. She swept into the living room, resisting the impulse to stand there with one hand on her hip.

Jack waved her to the couch. In front of it was the coffee-table, and on the coffee-table was tea, sandwiches and a small plate of salad. Miranda realised that she was indeed hungry.

He came over to her, took her arm and saw her to the couch. 'I did you a little extra in case you were really hungry,' he said. 'But do leave it if it's too much.' He was obviously determined to be the complete host, urbane, thoughtful—and distant. He sat in a chair opposite her.

He had changed, was now dressed casually in dark shirt and trousers. And when she looked at him, the tall muscular body, the expressive face, she felt that stirring of excitement that he always brought out in her. But why didn't he show that he was excited to see her?

She sat, took a sandwich. They were small, thin, delicate sandwiches and they were delicious. 'These are very dainty,' she said ungraciously. 'Did you make them?'

'I did indeed. I don't like taking great wads of bread, filling them with enough calories to feed a family and then cramming them into your mouth.'

Perhaps he had a point. And the sandwiches were delicious. She ate a couple more, drank some tea and then turned to fight.

'We were going to go to London,' she said. 'You were going to show me round. And there we were going to talk about our future.'

His voice was reluctant. 'Yes, I did say that. Perhaps we can go soon.' She thought that a certain tightening of his jaw muscles showed that he was not too keen on the idea.

'Jack, you need to have a wife who can give you babies. You know that, don't you?'

He didn't like the directness of the question. 'Not all men get what they want. Or women.'

'Well, I couldn't give you them before. But now— probably—I can. I don't know what Professor Laker told you, but when you came to see me there was still some doubt as to whether the operation had been a success. Jack, I had to wait four days until I had a proper examination and was told that, yes, things seemed to be fine. Four days of pain and doubt, Jack! I risked a lot, paid a lot to have this chance. And I did it—not entirely, but largely—for you. I would have expected a bit more concern, a bit more anything from you!'

Then she winced. She must still be a bit upset by the operation, she was being too hard on him.

And now he was angry. 'You did what you thought I wanted? Did you ask me? Did we talk about it? Haven't you been talking to me for the last few months about how necessary it is to consult, to decide things together? And you take this…this…this most important decision of your life without even mentioning it to me?'

'I thought that—'

'I doubt you did think. I could have helped, Miranda. How do you think I felt when I realised that Carly, my own sister, knew more about you than I did? I should have been told!'

'I did it so we could have a family!'

'Miranda, I've told you, told you, told you! It's you I wanted! I would marry you with or without the prospect of a family. It wasn't necessary to go…to go sneaking off like that.'

'You're angry because you had no part in planning this operation. You think you should have decided it yourself!' Her voice seemed to echo round the room.

He didn't answer, he just looked at her, and Miranda felt a thrill of dismay. She had gone too far and Jack was changing, right in front of her eyes. His face had shown anger, well, that was fine. She could deal with anger. But now his face was blank. Then there was that expression that she hated so much. The old, cold, self-contained Jack was back with a vengeance. The man who had no time for closeness. The man who saw her as a hospital worker, not a person.

'Would you like more tea?' he asked politely. 'And I could cut more sandwiches if you wish.'

She stared at him, appalled. 'Tea! Sandwiches! Jack, we're talking about our future here!'

He rose to his feet and said, 'I still want to be an adequate host. I'll fetch more tea and we can—'

'Sit down!' she snapped. Of course, he did no such thing.

Thinking quickly, desperately, she said in a quieter tone, 'Jack, please, sit down.'

Then he did. 'There's something you wanted to say?'

'Jack, the last time I sat on this couch you said you loved me. I didn't ask you to, it was your own decision to say it. And it made me happier than you can imagine.'

'If I remember rightly, first I said I thought I loved you. I was being honest, trying to be exact about my feelings. Afterwards, I guess I got carried away. Now, more tea?'

'No, thank you,' she said. After a pause she went on, 'You seemed very happy to get carried away. But, still, memories differ. Will you do something for me?'

'If I can.'

She was sitting at one end of his long leather couch, and she pointed to the other end. 'Go and sit at that end of the couch. Put your back against the arm and stretch your legs along the seat.'

'What? But why…? Are you trying to—?'

'I am your guest and I have just had quite a serious operation,' she reminded him. 'It doesn't seem much to ask.'

He did as she asked. Then, shakily, she stood and walked to his end of the couch. She sat between his legs, leaned her body back against his. 'Is there a point to this?' he asked.

'There is a point. Now, if you're comfortable, I'd like you to wrap your arms round me. Very gently, of course. Then I want us just to sit here in silence for ten minutes.'

'Thinking about what?'

'Not thinking at all. Just feeling. And perhaps remembering that we were like this when you said you…thought you…loved me.'

'Is this supposed to—?'

'Just be quiet and feel, Jack.'

Would this work? she wondered.

There was still some pain from her operation but she had learned to live with it and it diminished every day. She felt deep apprehension—would this work? Other than this, she was happy. Jack was comfortable to lie on. There was his own unmistakable smell, a combination of expensive aftershave and body warmth. There was the giving firmness of his muscles. There was the gentle in-and-out movement of his chest as he breathed.

For perhaps five minutes they sat there in silence together. Then she felt the tautness of his body relaxing. One of his hands moved further round her, grasped her two hands. His other hand reached for her face, a gentle finger caressed her ear, her cheek, ran across her lips. But nothing was said. There were five minutes to go.

'I think our ten minutes are up,' she said eventually, 'I'll move if you want me to.'

'No. I'm quite comfortable.' He craned his head, kissed her neck, and she shivered with delight.

'I've got something to tell you,' she said. 'I love you. You claim to be logical. But you're angry at me just because I did something without telling you, and it was something that you wanted. But I did it to make you—and me—happy.'

'You love me?' His voice seemed curious, as if he couldn't believe what she had just said.

'Of course I do. You can be irritating and sometimes you're stubborn. Sometimes you can be downright scary! But you're a good man, a fair man, and everyone respects that. And underneath your formidable exterior, you're very lovable.' She snuggled down, safe in the arms of the man she loved. 'Now, don't say anything to me. Just lie there and take things easy. I'm ill, remember. I have to be cosseted.'

He gently kissed the top of her head. 'I want to cosset you. Listen, Miranda, I don't know if it's this couch or this position but I want to repeat something I said before. I don't think I love you. I know I do. So…will you marry me?'

Miranda smiled. 'Of course I'll marry you,' she said. 'And I'll try to make you as happy as you'll make me.'

Jack looked lovingly at the woman who had transformed his life, his brave, beautiful, incredible Miranda who had risked so much, just for him. 'You make me happy just by being with me, you don't have to try. And whether we have a family or not, we'll certainly have each other. For ever and always.'

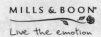

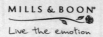

researching the cure

The facts you need to know:

- Breast cancer is the commonest form of cancer in the United Kingdom. **One woman in nine** will develop the disease during her lifetime.

- Each year around **41,000** women and approximately **300** men are diagnosed with breast cancer and around **13,000** women and **90** men will die from the disease.

- 80% of all breast cancers occur in post-menopausal women and approximately 8,200 pre-menopausal women are diagnosed with the disease each year.

- However, survival rates are improving, with on average 77.5% of women diagnosed between 1996 and 1999 still alive five years later, compared to 72.8% for women diagnosed between 1991 and 1996.

Breast Cancer Campaign is the only charity that specialises in funding independent breast cancer research throughout the UK. It aims to find the cure for breast cancer by funding research which looks at improving diagnosis and treatment of breast cancer, better understanding how it develops and ultimately either curing the disease or preventing it.

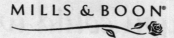

MILLS & BOON®

All you could want for Christmas!

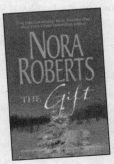

VC

4 FREE

BOOKS AND A SURPRISE GIFT!

We would like to take this opportunity to thank you for reading this Mills & Boon® book by offering you the chance to take FOUR more specially selected titles from the Medical Romance™ series absolutely FREE! We're also making this offer to introduce you to the benefits of the Mills & Boon® Reader Service™—

- ★ FREE home delivery
- ★ FREE gifts and competitions
- ★ FREE monthly Newsletter
- ★ Exclusive Reader Service offers
- ★ Books available before they're in the shops

Accepting these FREE books and gift places you under no obligation to buy, you may cancel at any time, even after receiving your free shipment. Simply complete your details below and return the entire page to the address below. You don't even need a stamp!

YES! Please send me 4 free Medical Romance books and a surprise gift. I understand that unless you hear from me, I will receive 6 superb new titles every month for just £2.80 each, postage and packing free. I am under no obligation to purchase any books and may cancel my subscription at any time. The free books and gift will be mine to keep in any case.

M6ZED

Ms/Mrs/Miss/Mr .... Initials ....

BLOCK CAPITALS PLEASE

Surname ....

Address ....

....

.... Postcode ....

Send this whole page to:
UK: FREEPOST CN81, Croydon, CR9 3WZ